The woman was still lying where Devlin had left her.

When he stopped beside the bed, he saw that her eyes were open. He'd grown so accustomed to her being unconscious that it was a shock to see her awake.

He'd turned on a lamp near the bed earlier, and in its light he could see that her eyes were large, their color hovering somewhere between blue and green. At another time he might have thought them beautiful. At the moment he was struck by their complete lack of expression.

She didn't seem at all disturbed to find herself in an unfamiliar bed. She stared at him for a long, silent moment. There was no visible change in her expression, nothing to tell him that she was glad he'd saved her life.

Something about that blank gaze made Devlin uneasy.

Who was Annalise St. John, and what had happened to drive all the life from her eyes?

Dear Reader,

When two people fall in love, the world is suddenly new and exciting, and it's that same excitement we bring to you in Silhouette Intimate Moments. These are stories with scope and grandeur. The characters lead lives we all dream of, and everything they do reflects the wonder of being in love.

Longer and more sensuous than most romances, Silhouette Intimate Moments novels take you away from everyday life and let you share the magic of love. Adventure, glamour, drama, even suspense— these are the passwords that let you into a world where love has a power beyond the ordinary, where the best authors in the field today create stories of love and commitment that will stay with you always.

In coming months, look for novels by your favorite authors: Kathleen Eagle, Marilyn Pappano, Emilie Richards, Judith Duncan and Justine Davis, to name only a few. And whenever—and wherever—you buy books, look for all the Silhouette Intimate Moments, love stories with that extra something, books written especially for you by today's top authors.

Leslie J. Wainger
Senior Editor and Editorial Coordinator

DALLAS SCHULZE

Everything but Marriage

SILHOUETTE·INTIMATE·MOMENTS®

Published by Silhouette Books New York

America's Publisher of Contemporary Romance

SILHOUETTE BOOKS
300 East 42nd St., New York, N.Y. 10017

EVERYTHING BUT MARRIAGE

ISBN: 0-373-07414-X

First Silhouette Books printing January 1992

Books by Dallas Schulze

Silhouette Intimate Moments

Moment to Moment #170
Donovan's Promise #247
The Vow #318
The Baby Bargain #377
Everything but Marriage #414

DALLAS SCHULZE

loves books, old movies, her husband and her cat, not necessarily in that order. She's a sucker for a happy ending, whose writing has given her an outlet for her imagination and hopes that readers have half as much fun with her books as she does! Dallas has more hobbies than there is space to list them, but is currently working on a doll collection.

To my editor Lucia Macro,
who's been a lot of fun to work with.

Prologue

"We find the defendant guilty."

Reed Hall felt the impact of the words strike the man standing beside him, but a quick glance showed absolutely no expression in Devlin Russell's face. He might have been listening to someone reading from a newspaper rather than hearing himself convicted of first-degree murder.

Reed listened to the sentencing, listened to the judge wipe out the next twenty years of a man's life. Devlin was twenty-two. After twenty years in prison, his youth would be gone, stolen not just by the years but by hard experience. If he survived.

Reed glanced at his client again. Something told him Devlin Russell would survive. There was no give in him. Reed didn't think prison was going to change that.

There was a buzz in the courtroom as the judge finished speaking. Reed turned to Devlin, speaking quickly before the guards came to remove the younger man.

"This isn't the end of it, Russell. We can appeal."

The eyes Devlin turned to him were steel gray and full of icy bitterness. "Save your breath, Hall. The evidence was overwhelming. You know it and I know it."

"It was circumstantial," Reed said stubbornly.

"And that's the only reason I'm not facing time on death row," Devlin said harshly. "Don't waste energy on me. Save it for the next poor bastard."

The guards stopped next to the table, and for an instant, Reed thought he saw a wild despair in Devlin's eyes. But it was gone so quickly he might have imagined it. Without another word, Devlin turned, holding out his hands for handcuffs to be snapped over his wrists.

Reed's gaze followed him as he was led from the courtroom. Devlin didn't look back. The attorney snapped his briefcase closed as the door shut behind his client. No one had ever told him that being a public defender was an easy task. He didn't expect it to be easy. In the five years he'd spent at the job, he thought he'd developed a certain hardness, a shell that was practically impenetrable.

But something about Devlin Russell had gotten through that shell. It wasn't anything Reed could put his finger on. There was certainly nothing soft or vulnerable about the young man. He hadn't made any extravagant claims to innocence.

He'd admitted to sleeping with his employer's young wife. He'd made no apologies for that. But he hadn't killed her. His eyes hadn't pleaded with Reed to believe him. In fact, he didn't really seem to give a damn what anybody thought, which hadn't helped him with the jury, Reed acknowledged with a sigh.

He lifted his briefcase, but his eyes lingered on the door through which they'd taken Devlin. He should drop this one. Devlin was right. The evidence against him had been overwhelming. He should just chalk this up as one of those things. You couldn't win them all. You had to learn to live with the failures.

The problem was, he believed Devlin Russell was innocent. How did you live with seeing an innocent man sent to prison?

Eight years later...

"You can tell his lawyers to take the money and burn it. I don't want it." Devlin Russell paced from one side of Reed's small office to the other.

"Think about it, Devlin," Reed suggested quietly. "I know how you feel but—"

"You *don't* know how I feel," Devlin interrupted harshly. "I just spent eight years in that hellhole. Eight years of my life gone forever. Eight years doing time for a crime I didn't commit.

"And now that old bastard thinks he can make up for it by leaving me his money. Well, nothing can make up for what he did to me."

"I didn't say it could." Reed leaned back in his desk chair, watching Devlin through narrowed eyes.

It was the first time he'd seen Devlin since he'd been released from prison less than a week before. Over the past eight years, Reed had made it a point to visit the other man. But seeing him outside the thick gray walls, he was struck by how much the years inside had changed Devlin.

Eight years ago, there'd still been traces of youth about him—a certain lankiness that hadn't yet disappeared, maybe a trace of softness around the mouth. But there was none of that now. The man in front of him was all hard muscle and barely contained anger.

"Think about it before you turn the money down," Reed said again.

"I don't want Sampson's money," Devlin said flatly. "Dead or alive, he can't buy my forgiveness. I hope he rots in hell."

"I don't think he was trying to buy your forgiveness. From what his lawyers told me, he was looking for forgiveness from a higher source." Reed's mouth twisted cynically.

"Eight years of my life gone. You can't wipe the slate clean that easily."

"Maybe not. Thankfully, that's not our decision." Reed tapped the small stack of papers in front of him. "When Harold Sampson made a deathbed confession to murdering his wife, he made you a free man.

His will makes you a very rich one. In the letter he dictated, he said that he couldn't die with your conviction on his conscience.''

"He didn't have much trouble living with it for eight years," Devlin said cynically.

"I'll admit that his sudden religious streak seems conveniently timed for him to meet his maker with a clear conscience, but that's not the point. The point is that you are now, not only exonerated of the crime, but independently wealthy.''

"I already told you I don't want his money."

"And I'll tell you again that I think you're cutting off your nose to spite Sampson's face. The money can't give you back the last eight years, but it can make the rest of your life a hell of a lot easier. If you don't take it, what are you going to do?

"A prison record, even on an unjust conviction, isn't likely to make most employers all that eager to hire you. What kind of a job do you think you'll get? Construction? Heavy labor? I'd think you'd have had enough of that."

Devlin's shoulders shifted uneasily under the cheap nylon jacket he was wearing. Despite himself, he was starting to listen to Reed's arguments. What the hell was he going to do with the rest of his life?

"You've got a sister somewhere up north, don't you?"

"Kelly," Devlin murmured. A cloudy image of a gap-toothed, eight-year-old came to mind. An entire decade had passed since he'd seen her. She'd be eighteen or nineteen now. He'd received letters from her over the years, though he stopped writing after he was arrested for Laura Sampson's murder.

"Well, think what the money could do for her," Reed suggested. "You could become something of a philanthropist if you'd like."

"I don't think I'm the philanthropist type."

"So spend it all on yourself. Don't look on this as money to buy your forgiveness, Devlin. Look on it as the least Sampson owed you. He stole eight years of your life. The money can't give that back to you, I know. But think about what it *can* do for you."

"What happens if I refuse it?"

"The courts will have to decide what to do with it. It will probably take years because there are no obvious heirs. The expenses will mount while the will lies frozen in probate, which will make a lot of lawyers very happy. Or you can save the courts a lot of time and accept it."

"Bloody hell." Devlin shoved his hands into the pockets of his jeans and turned to stare out the window. He'd been released less than two weeks ago, and he still hadn't quite gotten used to his freedom. The idea that he could not only look at the thick carpet of lawn across the street but actually go and walk on it if he chose was still hard to absorb.

If he didn't take the money, he was going to have to find work immediately, and he wasn't going to be able to be too choosy about what he took, either. One thing he knew, he couldn't ever work indoors again. He'd had enough of walls and closed doors to last him a lifetime.

If he took the money, he wouldn't have to worry about finding work. He could go see Kelly, go home. Not that there was much left for him in Indiana anymore. But Kelly was still there.

She was all the family he had, unless you counted his crazy old man, and Devlin hadn't counted him in a long time. With this money, he would be able to buy Kelly anything she wanted, take her anywhere she wished to go. He had a chance to make up for all the years he hadn't been there for her.

Listen to him. He was as bad as Sampson, thinking money could make up for lost time. But Reed was right. It could make life a lot easier from here on out. And he could always give the damn stuff away later.

"I'll take it," he said without turning from the window.

Reed stifled a grin and reached for the papers on his desk. The mills of the gods not only ground slow and fine, they ground out some pretty peculiar stuff. But it seemed as if they did get around to providing justice eventually.

Chapter 1

The building was little more than a shell—four walls and a roof. The exterior was still plywood, the interior contained only enough walls to provide structural support, and those walls were bare studs and exposed wiring.

Devlin Russell stood in the middle of the room that would eventually be the living room. Hands on his hips, he surveyed his new home, feeling satisfaction well up inside him. It was exactly the way he'd envisioned it.

He hadn't been sure he could explain what he wanted well enough for anyone to draw up usable plans. But Kelly's husband, Dan Remington, had suggested Michael Sinclair, and Michael had given him just what he'd asked for. Plenty of open space and lots of windows. The only doors would be on the bathroom and the closets. Other than that, one room flowed easily into the next.

Dan's company, Remington Construction, had put up the shell, but Devlin planned to do most of the remaining work himself. It paid to have relatives in the business.

The idea of having family was still new. When he'd come back to Remembrance last summer, he'd practically walked in on the middle of his sister's wedding. He'd found himself not only a brother-in-law, but about to become an uncle.

Thinking about his nephew, Clay Remington, aged nine months brought a rare smile to Devlin's lean features. He'd never thought of himself as particularly fond of children, but that was before he'd discovered his nephew's toothless smile.

Thunder cracked in the distance, breaking into his thoughts. A cool wind danced through the open doorway, smelling of rain. Devlin turned to face it, inhaling the damp scent as if it were a fine perfume. After eight years in prison, it was far more precious than any perfume.

If the scent could be bottled, it would sell for a fortune on the inside. Men who'd stab each other over a tube of toothpaste would have committed murder in the blink of an eye for just one breath of the air he was breathing now. Air that didn't smell of concrete and unwashed bodies, fear and despair.

He shook his head, forcing the memories back, locking them in a deep corner of his mind. That was behind him now. He was never going to be closed in again, never going to be shut away from the smell of rain and growing things.

Lightning flashed, an eye-searing bolt of white that lightened the twilight sky. Thunder crashed hard on its heels, bringing with it the near-silent rush of rain.

Without a moment's hesitation, Devlin walked outside, pulling the door shut behind him. Lightning split the sky again, so close he could almost smell the ozone. He thought briefly that it might be wiser to stay inside. But he'd spent too many years on the inside, too many years missing the clean feel of falling rain. Even after almost a year, being able to walk in the rain felt like something approaching a miracle.

He shoved his hands into the pockets of his jeans, circling around the house toward the overgrown field that only the most optimistic individual would have called a yard.

The rain fell in soft, heavy drops, soaking him to the skin in a matter of minutes. The earth drank in the moisture, sending up a dark, musty scent.

A river ran along the bottom of the field, one of the features that had persuaded Devlin to buy the property. The real estate agent had been careful to point out that the water was too deep and too swift at this particular spot to offer decent fishing. But Devlin wasn't interested in the fishing. He just liked the idea of having a stretch of free-flowing water practically at his back door.

He'd almost reached the riverbank when he realized he wasn't the only one foolish enough to come out in a rainstorm. Across the river from Devlin's property was another field and beyond that, a little-used country road. He guessed the other storm worshiper had left a car on the road and walked across the field, a long, soggy hike through knee-high grass and weeds.

The driving rain and the approaching darkness made it difficult to distinguish much more than a vague shape on the opposite bank. A woman, judging from the white dress she was wearing. She was coatless and bareheaded.

Standing too close to the edge of the bank, he thought critically, particularly with the ground soaking up the rain like it was. The ground near the edge of the river was less than stable, as evidenced by the muddy scars of innumerable small cave-ins.

Devlin started to call across to her, warn her that she was too close to the edge. But he shut his mouth without speaking. There was something in her posture that made it seem as if it would be an intolerable intrusion to speak to her.

She stood staring down at the water, her arms hanging loose at her sides, her shoulders hunched slightly forward as if bent under some burden. Something in the posture spoke to him through the careful walls he'd built around himself. Even through the driving rain, he recognized a soul deep in despair. He'd been there often enough himself to be able to see it in someone else.

He took a step back, thinking to leave her alone with her thoughts. But she was still too close to the edge of the river. Maybe she wasn't aware of it, couldn't see how unstable the bank was from where she stood.

"Hey!" She responded sluggishly to his call, her head lifting slowly, as if it were too heavy for her neck to support. Her face was a pale oval in the growing darkness, her eyes smudgy shadows.

Her despair seemed to reach across the yards that separated them, grabbing him by the throat, choking off the words of warning he'd intended to offer. She looked like a ghost, her pale face and hair taking on an otherworldly gleam in the rainy darkness.

For the space of several heartbeats, they stared at each other. Devlin blinked, forcing aside the fanciful idea that she was a figment of his imagination. She was just another lost soul. And she was standing too close to the edge of the river.

He started to call out to her again, to tell her to move back from the water. But before he could say anything, she moved, lifting one hand—toward him?

Afterward Devlin could never be sure what happened next. Did the bank crumble under her feet? Did she start to move back and lose her footing? Or did she quite deliberately step off the bank? The only thing he was sure of was that she didn't cry out. She tumbled into the rushing water as silently as if she were indeed nothing more than a figment of his imagination.

Even as the water closed over her, Devlin was wrenching his shoes off, letting them fall to the wet grass. Taking two running steps forward, he jumped off the bank after her.

He hit the water feet first, feeling the icy shock of it penetrate his jeans instantly. The current promptly tumbled him headfirst into the river. He surfaced, gasping for air, his arms flailing to keep his head above water.

He let the current sweep him along, squinting ahead for some sign of the woman. There. Only a few yards away, he caught a glimpse of something pale. He swam toward her, using the force of the current to help him.

She went under an instant before he reached her. Devlin launched himself forward, plunging his hands under the water where he'd seen her disappear. His left hand tangled in something soft and flowing, whether it was her hair or her dress, he couldn't tell. As he locked his fingers around it, the water took him under with a malicious gurgle.

He surfaced, gulping in air. One-handed, he floundered toward the edge of the river. The water was probably no more than chest deep, but the river narrowed here and the current was swift, making it impossible for him to get his feet under him for more than an instant at a time.

He grabbed hold of a tree root that protruded from the bank, pulling himself and his burden to the water's edge. So far, he'd felt no movement from the woman. She'd neither struggled against him nor aided his efforts. He wondered briefly if he was dragging a body out of the water, but there was no time to worry about it. Alive or dead, he wasn't leaving her in the river.

By the time he'd manhandled her limp form up onto the riverbank, he wasn't sure he had the energy to accomplish the same for himself. The river tugged at him, trying to drag him back under as he pulled himself out of its deceptively soft embrace.

Devlin collapsed onto the wet grass next to the woman, feeling the rain beating down on his back. It was coming in torrents now, making him wonder if they weren't just as likely to be drowned here as they had been in the river.

If she wasn't drowned already. The thought sent a spurt of energy through his tired muscles. Getting to his knees, he bent over her, pressing his fingers to her throat, seeking a pulse. He couldn't feel anything but her chilled skin.

His face grim, he ripped open her blouse and laid his ear against her chest. For a moment, he thought all his struggles had been in vain—that he'd accomplished nothing more than pulling a corpse from the rushing water. Then, so faint he almost dismissed it as his imagination, he heard a heartbeat.

Lifting his head, he watched her chest rise as she drew in a breath. She coughed weakly and he turned her onto her side, rubbing her back as she coughed up the river water she'd swallowed. What were you supposed to do for someone who'd almost drowned?

Her skin felt like ice beneath his hands. The first thing to do was to get her warm. Devlin lifted his head, peering through the rainy darkness, trying to orient himself. There were no lights to be seen. The storm clouds were so thick that no moonlight shone through.

He didn't know how far downstream the river had swept them. He shivered as a gust of wind blew the rain almost horizontally. The one thing he did know was that they needed to get some shelter and warmth.

Devlin got to his feet, pulling the woman up with him. She was limp in his hold, apparently unconscious. He bent, putting his shoulder against her midriff. Grunting with effort, he stood upright with her slung over his shoulder.

Unless the current had swept them a great deal farther than he thought likely, the house was the nearest shelter to be found.

He put his head down and started walking.

One thing eight years in prison had taught him was endurance. And determination. He didn't think about how tired he was or how far he might have to walk. He didn't think about the stones that bruised his bare feet. And he never considered the possibility that his strength might give out.

He simply walked steadily forward, using the sound of the river as a guide to make sure he didn't wander too far off his path. He'd left a light on in the kitchen. Another hundred steps and he'd be able to see it. And if not, then he'd take a hundred more and a hundred beyond that, if necessary.

The woman was a dead weight on his shoulder. He could feel her arms swing limply against his back with each step he took. He could only assume that she was still breathing.

His legs were beginning to tremble with exhaustion. Devlin lifted his head, peering through the rain.

Was that a light, or was it his imagination that put it there? He took a few more steps but the light remained steady. The sight of it poured new strength into him.

Veering away from the river, he kept his eyes on the light, half afraid it might vanish as he drew closer. But it didn't vanish, and he could make out the sturdy outline of the house.

Pushing open the back door, Devlin stumbled inside. He leaned against the wall for a moment, savoring the feeling of being in and out of the rain and darkness. If he'd been alone, he would have let himself slide down the wall and collapse in a heap on the floor.

But he wasn't alone. Besides, now that he was inside, he could feel a bone-deep chill. They both needed to get warm.

Forcing his aching legs to move again, he carried his burden into the bathroom, the one room in the house that was completely finished. He bent, letting her slide off his shoulder, his hands guiding her to the floor. Stepping over her limp body, he turned the water on in the shower stall, testing it cautiously until he was sure he wasn't going to scald both of them.

Once the temperature was adjusted to his satisfaction, he turned his attention to his unknown guest. Kneeling beside her on the tile floor, he began stripping her clothes off. She was breathing but still unconscious. He didn't know if that was a bad sign or not, but he did know that she needed to get warm.

She was too thin, he noted absently. Her ribs were plainly visible along her side, and her hipbones were much too prominent. Her hair was long, pulled back by a rubber band that had survived her tumble into the river. Devlin snapped it, feeling the heavy wet strands spill over his hands.

Once he had her naked, he stood and stripped off his jeans and shirt. He hesitated over his briefs, wondering how she'd react if she regained consciousness to find herself locked in a shower stall with a naked man. On the other hand, the briefs were cold and wet and hardly enough to reassure a frightened woman. Shrugging, he stepped out of them, dropping them onto the floor with the rest of their clothing.

Bending, he picked the woman up. Elbowing open the shower door, he stepped beneath the warm spray with her in his arms. The water sluiced over them. Devlin lowered her feet to the floor, sliding one arm around her waist to support her against his body.

Under other circumstances, it could have been a highly erotic moment. A man and a woman naked in the shower together could hardly be anything else. Unless of course, both of them were chilled to the bone and one of them was unconscious.

Devlin kept them both under the water until he felt warm again. The woman had stirred once or twice, her features puckering as if she felt the pain of returning warmth. But she didn't wake up. Devlin had the odd feeling that she didn't particularly want to wake up.

He turned the water off and lifted her out of the shower stall, holding her braced against his hip while he reached for a towel to wrap around her. Grabbing another towel for himself, he lifted her against his chest and carried her into the bedroom.

Since furniture hadn't been a major priority up until now, his bed was the only place he could put her. He set her on the mattress, easing the towel away before pulling the sheet and blanket up over her. Clumsily he wrapped the towel around her hair, thinking it would be better than letting it soak the pillow.

He toweled himself dry and pulled on fresh jeans and a sweatshirt before returning to stare down at his guest. Who was she? Had she fallen into the river or jumped? Remembering those seconds before she'd disappeared into the water, Devlin couldn't be sure which it had been. Was she going to thank him for saving her life or curse him?

Shrugging, he found a heavy sweatshirt and sat down next to her on the bed. Whether she liked it or not, she was alive. And he had no intention of damn near getting himself killed fishing her out of the river only to see her catch pneumonia.

Easing her into a sitting position, he pulled the sweatshirt over her head, stuffing her arms into the sleeves, lifting her to pull the hem down over her hips. It was miles too big for her, in length as well as width, covering her past her thighs.

He noticed again how thin she was and wondered if she was making a fashion statement or simply hadn't been able to eat. No money?

He took the damp towel from her hair and wrapped the heavy length in a dry one. From the length of it, he guessed it would fall past her waist, and he found himself wondering what color it would be when it dried.

When he stood up, he noticed the bloodstains he'd left on the floor everywhere he walked. He hadn't realized his feet were bleeding until he saw the smears of red. He remembered feeling stones biting into his feet on the walk home, although after the first ten yards, he'd stopped noticing the pain, concentrating all his thoughts on moving forward.

Now that he had a chance to think about it, his feet hurt like hell. Devlin went into the bathroom and examined the bottoms of his feet. For the most part the cuts were small, but there were quite a few of them. He put bandages on one or two larger cuts and then pulled on a pair of heavy white socks.

Leaving the woman sleeping in his bed, he went out to the kitchen and put water on for coffee. While it heated, he used a towel to mop up the water he'd tracked through the house earlier. His feet had bled everywhere he walked, leaving stains on the floor. But since it was nothing but a plywood subfloor, Devlin wasn't concerned. Carpet and oak flooring would cover the marks eventually.

His guest still hadn't stirred by the time the coffee was ready. Devlin checked her pulse. It was steady, but did it seem a little too fast? Too shallow, maybe? She should probably see a doctor. For all he knew, there was something wrong with her besides being too thin and, what, judging by the smudgy shadows under her eyes, he'd guessed was a pretty bad case of exhaustion.

He could put her in the car and take her into town, drop her off at the emergency room and wash his hands of her. But wouldn't she be terrified to wake up in a hospital, surrounded by strangers?

"Yeah, right, Russell. Like she knows you so well," he muttered aloud. Still, something in him resisted the idea of taking her to the hospital.

Before he could make a decision, the soft chimes of the doorbell broke into his thoughts. Giving his visitor a last glance, he left the bedroom. He was too far off the beaten track to get many unexpected visitors. His sister Kelly was the only person who might drop in on him, and she wasn't likely to have driven so far out in the middle of a storm.

Devlin pulled the door open, staring blankly at the man on the doorstep. His thoughts had been so caught up in the woman in his bedroom, it took him a second to shift his focus and realize who he was looking at.

'Ben.'

Ben's smile took on a quizzical edge. "Have I got the wrong night? I thought you asked me to come out tonight."

"Tonight." Devlin shook his head, his mouth twisting in a smile. "No, you don't have the wrong night. I'd forgotten. Come in."

"I could come back another time," Ben offered.

"No. This is fine. In fact, your timing is great."

Devlin took Ben's wet coat and hung it up on one of the nails that served as a coat hook until he could get around to putting a real coat closet in.

"Everyone tells me that," Ben commented, following Devlin into the kitchen. He nodded in answer to Devlin's offer of coffee. "Why is my timing particularly great this time?"

"I have a problem." Devlin handed him a cup of coffee. He'd forgotten all about asking Ben Masters to come see him. *Dr.* Ben Masters. He'd planned on discussing a donation to the clinic that was Ben's pet project, but the other man's arrival was too fortuitous to ignore.

"Problems are my medical specialty," Ben said.

"There's a woman in my bedroom."

Ben's brows rose. "We should all have such problems."

"Yeah, well this one really is a problem. I fished her out of the river earlier tonight. She seems okay, but she hasn't regained consciousness."

"Any sign of a head injury?" Ben asked, all traces of flippancy gone. He was suddenly the complete professional.

"None that I can see."

"How long was she in the water?"

"Not long before I got to her and pulled her head up. It took a little while longer to get both of us out of the water. And it was a while after that before I got her home. She was cold, so I put her in a warm shower and then put her in bed."

"Sounds good so far. I'd like to see her."

"Be my guest." Devlin circled the breakfast bar and led the way into the bedroom.

The woman was still lying where he'd left her, but when he stopped beside the bed, he saw that her eyes were open. He'd grown so accustomed to her being unconscious that it was a shock to see her awake.

He'd turned on a lamp near the bed earlier, and in its light, he could see that her eyes were large, the color hovering somewhere between blue and green. At another time, he might have thought them beautiful. At the moment, he was struck by their complete lack of expression.

She didn't seem at all disturbed to find herself in an unfamiliar bed, with two strange men standing over her. She stared at him for a long, silent moment before her eyes shifted over his shoulder to Ben. She gave him the same silent scrutiny and then closed her eyes as if losing interest in keeping them open.

It was left to Ben to speak. Something in that wide blue-green gaze had left Devlin voiceless. He stepped back automatically as Ben edged by him and sat on the side of the bed. The woman's eyes opened again as she felt the bed dip, but she only stared at Ben with that same emptiness in her eyes.

"Hi. How are you feeling?" Ben's voice was low and soothing. He reached for her arm, which was lying on top of the covers, his fingers searching for her pulse. She watched him for a moment, as if debating whether or not to answer him.

"I'm okay," she said at last. Her voice was so low Devlin had to strain to hear it.

"Good. Do you remember your name?"

"Annalise," she said slowly, frowning as if it were an effort to remember. "Annalise St. John."

"Do you remember falling in the river a little while ago?"

"No."

"Devlin pulled you out." Ben gestured over his shoulder to where Devlin stood silently watching. Her gaze shifted to Devlin, but there was no visible change in her expression, nothing to tell Devlin that she was glad he'd saved her life.

"I'm Ben Masters and I'm a doctor," Ben continued when she offered no response. "Would you mind if I checked you over? Made sure everything was in working order?" His friendly smile got no response. Her thin shoulders lifted in a gesture of indifference.

Taking that for consent, Ben glanced at Devlin. "Can you get my bag? It's in the front seat."

"Sure." Devlin left, glad of an excuse to leave the room. Something about that blank gaze made him uneasy. It was like looking at someone whose soul had abandoned her.

Who was Annalise St. John, and what had happened to drive all the life from her eyes?

Chapter 2

"Well, it would be a good idea to run a few tests—a blood workup, maybe. But I don't think there's anything physically wrong with her that about a week's worth of sleep and three square meals a day won't fix."

Ben and Devlin were seated at the breakfast bar, fresh mugs of coffee in front of them. Outside, the rain had gone from a downpour to a steady drizzle that slanted past the windows.

Annalise St. John was asleep again. She'd allowed Ben to examine her and then drifted off to sleep, apparently indifferent to his findings.

"So what's wrong with her?" Devlin asked, cradling his palms around his coffee.

"She's exhausted and undernourished. Could be anorexia," he said, more to himself than Devlin. He shook his head. "I don't think that's it, though. If I had to guess—which I do—I'd say she either hasn't had the money for food or doesn't care enough to bother eating."

"Doesn't care enough?" Devlin raised his brows. "I'd never really thought of food as something you had to care about to eat."

"Well, I can't be sure without seeing more of her, but I'd say your Annalise has a pretty nasty case of depression."

Devlin nearly protested Ben designating her as "his" Annalise, but it wasn't important enough to argue. "Depressed enough to commit suicide?" he asked slowly, remembering those moments when she'd stood on the riverbank across from him.

Ben shot him a quick look, his dark eyes sharp with interest. "Hard to say. Depression affects different people different ways. She seems very passive now, too passive to bother killing herself, I'd say. But that's not to say it's not possible. Is that what you think happened? She jumped in the river?"

"I don't know." Devlin lifted his shoulder in a shrug, half sorry he'd mentioned the possibility. It seemed like an intrusion into her privacy somehow. "It was getting dark, and the rain made it nearly impossible to see."

"Well, no one could say for sure but Annalise, and I'm not even sure she'd remember. She doesn't seem to remember much of anything."

"Amnesia?" Devlin questioned, startled.

"No. More like an immense indifference. Or maybe she thought I was being too nosy for my own good," he added with a grin.

Devlin's smile was perfunctory. Remembering those empty eyes, he didn't think Annalise cared what questions Ben asked. He didn't think she cared about anything.

"I can arrange to have her admitted to the hospital," Ben said briskly.

"The hospital? I thought you said there was nothing physically wrong with her."

"Depression is a treatable medical condition," Ben said.

"So she needs drugs or therapy to recover?"

"Not necessarily. There's no one treatment for depression. We'd have to do some testing. Hopefully, we could get some cooperation from her."

"Did you suggest this to her?"

"She fell asleep on me before I could mention it."

Devlin frowned down into his coffee cup. Ben was offering the obvious solution. Annalise St. John would be taken off his hands, given into the care of competent professionals who could help her deal with her problems. He could forget all about her and get on with finishing his house.

"I think I'll just let her sleep here tonight," he said slowly. "If she wants to go to the hospital tomorrow, I'll bring her in."

"Okay. Let me know how she's doing one way or another and don't hesitate to call if you need me." He drank the last of his coffee and slid off the high stool. "I've got early appointments in the morning so I'm going to head home. I'll give you a call tomorrow."

"Yeah. Thanks." Devlin stood up and held out his hand. "Thanks for everything. Send me a bill."

"I will." Ben grinned. "I make it a point to send bills to patients I figure can pay them."

"That reminds me," Devlin said, remembering the reason he'd asked Ben to come out in the first place. "I wanted to give you a check for your clinic. Kelly tells me you're doing some really worthwhile work."

"Kelly's prejudiced because she works there part-time," Ben said lightly, watching as Devlin dug through a drawer full of screwdrivers, cupboard handles and screws of assorted sizes until he finally came up with a checkbook.

"I feel we're doing some good," he continued. "People don't think of the poor as being a problem in a small town. But Rememberance has grown a lot in the last few years, and the problems have grown along with the town."

"Well, I've been hard up against it in my time," Devlin said, ripping the check out and handing it to Ben.

"Thanks. I really appreciate this." Ben's voice trailed off, his eyes widening in shock as he took in the size of the check. He looked at Devlin. "I was about to say that every little bit helps," he said with a shaken laugh. "But this definitely qualifies as more than a little bit. Thank you."

Devlin shrugged, wishing that he'd just made the donation anonymously, as he'd done with the other donations he'd made to various charities this past year. Maybe it was because he knew Ben through Kelly that he'd felt the urge to give him the check personally. Besides, Kelly had told him the clinic needed money urgently, and arranging anonymous donations took a little time.

"I'd appreciate it if you don't mention this to anyone. Including Kelly." Especially Kelly, he thought. The last thing he wanted was for her to start asking questions about how he came to have that kind of money to give away.

"Sure." Ben folded the check and slipped it into his pocket. "I really appreciate this. To tell the truth, I was wondering how we were going to pay the lease next week. This should take care of that worry for quite a while."

Devlin shrugged, ignoring the curiosity in the other man's eyes. "Like I said, I've been up against it a time or two myself."

He shut the door behind Ben, leaving his hand on the knob as he listened to the sound of Ben's rickety old sedan disappearing down the long driveway toward the road. From the condition of the doctor's car, he thought that perhaps he should have given him a donation toward a vehicle fund.

He hoped he hadn't misjudged Ben's discretion. He hadn't told his younger sister much of what he'd done since leaving home ten years before, turning her questions aside with vague answers about traveling a lot and offering thin excuses for why he hadn't written.

She'd finally stopped asking, glad enough to have him back in her life that she was willing to accept him without question. Devlin didn't need anyone to tell him that her husband didn't feel quite the same. Dan had never said anything, but it was obvious that he hadn't bought Devlin's vague explanations.

As far as Dan was concerned, there was no excuse for the way Devlin had simply disappeared from his sister's life, ignoring the letters, leaving her to deal with their mother's death and their father's abuse.

Looking at it from Dan's point of view, Devlin couldn't blame him for feeling the way he did. The fact that he hadn't known Seth Russell was abusing Kelly didn't excuse him, even in his own eyes. He *should* have known. He should have been able to read between the lines of Kelly's letters and see what was happening.

He shrugged, as if the physical gesture could ease the invisible burden of his thoughts. He couldn't have done anything to help Kelly even if he had known, but it didn't change the guilt he felt that he hadn't been there for her.

But the past was the past and he had other, more urgent concerns at the moment. Like an unconscious woman with possible suicidal tendencies. And the fact that he hadn't eaten since lunch, which was nearly eight hours ago.

If the former was a problem with no immediate solution, the latter was at least easily dealt with. Getting some leftover stew out of the refrigerator, he placed it on the stove and turned the burner to a low heat before going to check on his guest.

She didn't stir when Devlin stopped beside the bed. If it hadn't been for the barely perceptible rise and fall of her breathing, he would have been convinced that she was dead.

His hands in his pockets, Devlin looked down at her. There was nothing to be read from her features, nothing to tell him whether her fall into the river had been deliberate or accidental. Not that he'd expected a visible sign.

Annalise St. John. It was a pretty name—unusual. If he hadn't been there to pull her out of the river, would anyone have known what name to put on the body? Or would she simply have been buried in some graveyard, records of her death filed under the name Jane Doe? And would anyone have cared, one way or another, including her?

She was too thin. Her pale skin was stretched taut over cheekbones that were too sharp. One arm lay on top of the blanket, and the bones in her wrist were clearly visible. He pulled one hand out of his pocket and reached down to circle her wrist, frowning when he saw how much his finger overlapped his thumb.

How long had it been since she'd eaten a decent meal? She'd had nothing with her but the clothes on her back—no purse, no jewelry, no identification. Maybe she was one of the growing number of homeless, unable to find work, slipping through the cracks in the welfare system.

Her skin was cool to the touch. Only the faint but steady beat of her pulse under his finger reminded him that he was touching a living, breathing woman and not a pale statue.

How had she gotten out here, so far from town? It didn't seem likely that she'd walked this far. Unless she'd caught a ride from someone. Or maybe his original speculation had been right. She'd left a car somewhere across the river. Tomorrow he'd go look for it, tow it back here if necessary.

He released her arm, straightening slowly, his eyes still on her face. She was fine boned. Even with the added pounds she should be carrying, he suspected she'd have a fragile look about her. Was she attractive? He tilted his head, trying to picture her with a little more flesh on her bones, a touch of color in her cheeks.

But the image wouldn't quite come into focus. He kept seeing those blue-green eyes, completely empty of expression.

He'd seen a lot of misery during his time in prison. His first cell mate had hung himself a year after Devlin arrived. But he couldn't remember seeing quite that same emptiness in Sal's eyes before he killed himself.

He shrugged the memories off and turned away from the bed. Whatever had happened to bring the woman to this low, it wasn't his problem. He'd fished her out of the river, given her a place to spend the night.

In the morning, he'd feed her breakfast and take her to the hospital or any other place she wanted to go.

He'd provide her with money for a fresh start if that was what she needed. Money was the one thing he had plenty of these days. But that was as deep as his involvement was going to go.

Devlin ate the reheated stew, listening to the light patter of the rain on the roof. The weather report on the radio was promising clear skies by morning, which meant he could start on the redwood shingles that would cover the exterior of the house. And if the rain continued, there were plenty of things that needed doing inside. That was the thing about building a house, there was always work to do.

By the time he'd finished rinsing off his plate, the rain had stopped. Looking out the window over the sink, he could get an occasional glimpse of stars through the tattered cloud cover. That meant he'd be able to work outside tomorrow.

After he'd gotten the St. John woman settled, he reminded himself. He felt a mild twinge of annoyance. One thing he'd done his best to avoid, in the year since he'd left prison, was involvements of any sort.

He hadn't sought out friendships, hadn't gone looking for female companionship to ease an occasional endless night. Bitter experience had taught him that such ties, no matter how fleeting they were, could extract a higher price than he wanted to pay. Bedding Laura Sampson had cost him eight years of his life.

Not that he expected every such experience to end in a prison sentence. But it lingered in the back of his mind that he'd paid a high price for indulging a fleeting sexual urge.

It wasn't just sexual involvement he'd avoided. He'd even kept a certain distance from Kelly. She didn't know where he'd been or what he'd done in the years since he left home, and Devlin preferred to keep it that way. It was enough that he was back in her life.

Reed Hall was as close to a friend as he had. The lawyer had believed in him during the trial and had visited him despite Devlin's lack of encouragement. Reed had helped him get his bearings when he was released. But he couldn't let his guard drop completely, even with Reed.

The reserve that had been a part of him even before the trial, the wariness that was a partial legacy of his childhood, had hardened into a thick wall during his years in prison. Sometimes Devlin wondered if it was even possible to get through that wall. Cynically he doubted it was worth trying.

But apparently, you couldn't lock the world out completely, no matter how hard you tried. The world, in the form of one Annalise St. John, had arrived more or less on his doorstep.

He sighed, reaching up one hand to rub the back of his neck. By this time tomorrow, she'd be gone. He'd get her settled somewhere else first thing in the morning. Soon she'd be nothing more than a quickly fading memory. An anecdote he'd probably never tell anyone.

But at the moment she was occupying his bed, the only bed in the half-finished house. Which meant that he was going to have to find somewhere else to sleep.

An hour later, Devlin crawled into the sleeping bag he'd unrolled on the living room floor. With an air mattress under it, it made an adequate if not luxurious bed. Before he got the bed his unexpected guest was now occupying, he'd spent several weeks sleeping just like this, unrolling the sleeping bag in whichever room was least cluttered with construction debris.

Stretching out on his back, he linked his hands beneath his head and stared up at the open beams above him. He was tired. A full day's work followed by rescuing a woman from the river had left his body more than ready for a solid night's sleep. But his mind wasn't in the mood to cooperate.

His thoughts kept drifting to the woman in the next room. Who was she? He knew her name, but he didn't know anything else about her. How old was she? Somewhere in her twenties, maybe. Certainly not more than thirty. Just what had happened to drive all the life from her eyes?

It was none of his business, he reminded himself firmly. She was simply passing through his life. A week from now, he wouldn't even be able to remember her name. But he wondered how long it would take to forget those eyes. They followed him into sleep, their very emptiness asking for something he could never give.

* * *

Devlin had no idea what time it was when he woke. One thing his years in prison had taught him was the ability to go from sleep to fully awake in the blink of an eye. Sometimes your life could depend on how quickly you woke up.

His eyes snapped open, one hand groping for the crude knife that had rarely been far from his side during his years of incarceration. His fingers found nothing but the soft flannel of the sleeping bag. He blinked and drew in a quick breath. The clean scent of damp wood and open space banished the remembered mustiness of a prison cell.

His fingers relaxed and he breathed in again, slower and deeper this time. Whatever had awakened him, it wasn't immediately life threatening. He sat up, pushing the top layer of the sleeping bag away, listening to the night sounds.

There was nothing out of the ordinary. Crickets scratched out a mating call. Close by, an owl hooted, a lonely sound.

And somewhere, the sound of someone crying softly.

Devlin pushed the sleeping bag aside and stood up. The soles of his feet sent up an annoyed protest at being put to use again, but he ignored the discomfort. He'd left his jeans on when he went to bed but removed his shirt, and the air was cool against his bare chest. The crying had stopped by the time he reached the bedroom and he hesitated in the doorway.

She was still in bed. There was just enough light to make out the shape of her under the covers. As far as he could tell, she hadn't moved since the last time he'd looked in on her.

Maybe he should just go back to bed. It wasn't likely she'd want some stranger intruding on her. Devlin's fingers tightened over the edge of the doorway as the soft sobbing started again.

Go back to bed. It's not your problem. Mind your own business.

But he couldn't turn away. There was something so completely hopeless in the sound of her tears. It tugged at emotions he'd thought beaten out of him a long time ago.

She was nothing to him. A stranger. Tomorrow she'd be gone, and the day after, forgotten. Whatever her sorrows, they were nothing to do with him.

His knuckles turned white with strain as he stood in the doorway. The sound of her crying brought back all the empty, frightened nights he'd spent in his life. Starting when he was a boy, lying in bed, smarting from the bite of his father's belt and gritting his teeth against the tears he was too stubborn to shed.

He knew what it was to be alone, to feel hopeless. He'd felt the despair he could hear in her tears. And he couldn't just walk away and leave her alone.

His movements stiff, Devlin crossed the room to the bed. She seemed unaware that she was no longer alone. The quiet crying continued. He half expected her to tell him to go away. The sort of grief expressed in her tears was not the sort that invited company.

But she said nothing when he stopped beside the bed, made no acknowledgment of his presence. In the moonlight that filtered through the dissipating cloud cover, Devlin understood why.

She was still asleep. Her face was twisted with anguish, her fingers knotted on the light blanket, but her eyes were closed and it was obvious that she was not awake.

Devlin reached out to wake her but drew his hand back without touching her. Somehow, knowing that she was asleep made her tears seem more poignant. Her pain must run very deep to follow her past the boundaries of sleep.

Hardly knowing why he did it, Devlin found himself bending to gather her slight figure up off the bed. Blanket and all, he lifted her into his arms. The sobbing stopped on a caught breath. He waited for her to wake, perhaps frightened or angry at finding herself held by a strange man.

But she didn't wake. After a moment's stillness, she turned her face into his collarbone, her thin body relaxing in his hold. One hand came up to rest against his bare chest, her fingers cool on his skin. There was so much trust in the small movement that Devlin felt a quick catch in his heartbeat. His arms tightened protectively around her.

"Fool," he whispered. She didn't know whose arms were around her. She didn't know him at all. Perhaps she sensed that she was no longer alone, but it didn't matter whether it was Devlin Russell who held her or Joe Smith.

Cursing the soft streak that should have been
smothered years ago, Devlin eased down onto the bed
with her still in his arms. She didn't wake as he
bunched the pillows up behind his back. In fact, she
simply relaxed more fully, her breathing deeper now,
though still shaken by an occasional half sob.

Devlin leaned his head back against the wall and
stared into the darkness. Twenty-four hours ago, he'd
never heard of Annalise St. John. Twenty-four hours
from now, she'd be out of his life forever and forgotten soon after that. But for now, he was willing to
stand between her and whatever darkness was threatening her.

Chapter 3

Annalise woke slowly, aware of the soft comfort of clean sheets, the warmth of sunshine spilling across the bed. It had been weeks since she'd slept in a real bed. She felt a vague curiosity about her surroundings, but it faded before it could really take hold.

Her eyes still closed, she tried to retreat back into the comfort of sleep, but her body wouldn't cooperate. She was awake, whether she liked it or not. Not that it made an enormous difference. Awake or asleep, the world felt more or less the same.

She opened her eyes and stared up at the open beams above her. Open as in unfinished ceilings, she noted, her gaze skimming over the unfinished plywood and two-by-fours. The walls were in the same condition. Wherever she was, the building, or at least this room, was still under construction.

Vaguely she was aware that she should feel some curiosity about where she was and how she'd come to be there. With very little interest, she cast her thoughts back to the last thing she remembered. It wasn't much. Her car had died on a country road.

She'd left it and started walking. Like everything else lately, it hadn't seemed to matter whether or not her car ran. She hadn't been going to or coming from anywhere.

There'd been a storm. She could remember the rain soaking her clothes. Then she'd been inside—in this bed, perhaps?—and there'd been a man—or was it two?

Her tentative interest faded and she let the faint memories go. What difference did it make anyway? Yesterday paled into the same gray mist that had filled most of her days since—

No. She wasn't going to think about that. The hurt still lay under that soothing gray curtain, waiting to jump out at her. It would swallow her whole if it could. She wouldn't think about it. Better if she thought of nothing at all. That was safest.

Annalise sat up and swung her legs off the bed. Her head swam momentarily and she closed her eyes until the sensation abated. She frowned. She didn't like it when she felt things. Not even physical things, like dizziness. It was best not to think, not to feel.

Opening her eyes, she stared at the room without much interest. That it was a bedroom could be assumed from the presence of the bed she sat on. Beyond that, it was mainly bare walls and huge windows. There was an archway that led to a hall on one side of the room. On the other was a door, the only one in sight. She assumed that led to a bathroom.

She was wearing a man's sweatshirt beneath the sheets, her clothes nowhere in sight. She didn't wonder how she'd come to be that way. Whoever had put her in the big bed had obviously done her no harm. There was a white terry bathrobe draped across the foot of the bed and Annalise reached for it.

She'd just as soon stay where she was, but she doubted she'd be left alone for long. Experience told her that someone always came along, poking and prodding, asking her how she felt, wanting to know what she was thinking. She'd learned to avoid the county shelters for just that reason. It was easier to sleep in her car than to have to deal with all the questions and concerned looks.

The robe was large enough to go twice around her thin body. The hem dragged on the floor around her feet. It had been a long time since she'd concerned herself with how she looked. She cinched the belt tightly about her waist, pulling her thick hair out of the collar to let it straggle down her back.

Once the robe was secured, she hesitated over what to do next. What would she be expected to do? She puzzled over that for a moment. It was important to act like other people. If you acted different, it drew attention. And it was best not to draw attention.

She could smell coffee. She followed the scent toward the archway, her step reduced to an awkward shuffle by the hem of the robe.

* * *

A sixth sense had told Devlin his guest was awake even before she appeared across the breakfast bar from where he was sitting. Though it was barely eight o'clock, he'd been up since five. He'd had three hours to convince himself that the woman sleeping in his bed—who'd spent a good portion of the night in his arms—was nothing more than a minor inconvenience in his life. As soon as she woke, he'd find out where she'd come from or where she'd been going and see her on her way. End of story.

Which didn't explain the odd tightness he felt in his chest when he heard her stirring in the bedroom. He scowled at the book he'd been reading over breakfast. He'd found the biography of Catherine the Great quite enough to absorb his attention until now. Suddenly, a long-dead empress couldn't keep his attention from drifting to the waif he'd fished out of the river the night before.

He knew the precise instant that she left the bedroom, but he didn't lift his head from the book. He'd had plenty of time to familiarize himself with his guest's features over the past twelve hours or so, still he was reluctant to see her awake. Alive. It might make her real in a way he'd prefer not to see. He didn't want to see her as a real person. It was much simpler to view her as a package he had temporary care of.

He couldn't just pretend she wasn't there. Devlin lifted his head slowly as she stopped on the other side of the breakfast bar. His robe was ludicrously big on her. It wrapped around her thin torso more like a blanket than a garment. One side had slipped down to reveal her collarbone. There was something very vulnerable about that wedge of pale skin covering the too-prominent bone.

His eyes lifted to her face. He realized he'd made a mistake in assuming that seeing her awake and conscious was the same as seeing her *alive*. Except for the fact that her eyes were open, her face was the same pale, emotionless oval it had been.

The eyes that should have given her features life were just as empty as they had been the night before when Ben Masters had been here. They were blue-green, widely spaced and thickly lashed. The kind of eyes a man could drown in.

He'd heard that one's eyes were windows to their soul, revealing who the person was. Annalise St. John's eyes were nothing but beautiful mirrors, reflecting only his own image back at him.

He blinked and drew his eyes away, uncomfortable under that expressionless gaze.

"Have some coffee," he said, by way of greeting. He reached out to snag the pot. He lifted a cup off the rack that sat on the tiled bar and poured it full of steaming black brew, pushing it toward her. "Black okay?"

"Yes." She stared at the cup as if not quite certain what to do with it.

"Pull up a stool," Devlin suggested. She did as he suggested, pulling a stool from under the counter and sitting down across from him. He waited, but she didn't say anything. She just sat there, her hands in her lap, her eyes on the coffee cup.

"I've got tea, if you'd prefer it," he said, when the silence had stretched.

She reacted slowly, lifting her head to stare at him with those beautiful, expressionless eyes. "Coffee is fine."

She reached for the cup, lifting it to take a sip. He had the feeling she'd taken a drink more because he seemed to expect it rather than because she had any interest in the coffee.

"How are you feeling?"

"I'm fine, thank you."

"You could have taken a chill," Devlin said, watching for some reaction.

"I'm fine," she repeated as if it were a phrase she'd learned from an English translation book.

"From the river, I mean."

"River?" The word rose at the end, indicating a question, but there was no flicker of interest in those smooth features.

"Don't you remember?"

"I'm not sure." This time, her look was wary. It made him think of a small animal who'd learned to suspect a trap close on the heels of any kindness.

"You fell in the river yesterday. Last night, really. Or you jumped," he added deliberately, thinking to spark some reaction.

But she only blinked slowly, digesting his words as if they were about someone else. "I don't remember."

It was left to Devlin to interpret just what it was she didn't remember. Did she not remember being in the water at all? Or not remember whether she'd jumped?

"I pulled you out."

"Oh. Thank you," she added politely.

And that seemed to be the extent of her interest in the whole subject. Devlin wanted to take her by the shoulders and shake her out of the apathy that seemed to have swallowed every spark of life in her.

He wanted to call Ben and tell him to come get Ms. Annalise St. John. Take her to the hospital. Take her and sell her to white slavers. He just wanted her off his hands and out of his life. He didn't need the kind of aggravation she provided. He didn't need anything or anyone disturbing the hard-won tranquility he'd achieved in his life.

"You look like you could use something to eat," he said abruptly.

He got up without waiting for a response, if she had one. It was obvious that, for the moment at least, the best way to deal with his houseguest was to simply take charge. He didn't know whether she'd ever been capable of making decisions, but she didn't show any ability in that direction right now.

He'd get some food into her and then decide what the next step should be. One thing was certain, he wanted her off his hands as soon as possible.

Annalise dabbled her spoon in the bowl of hot cereal Devlin sat in front of her. He'd told her his name while he was preparing the cereal. Maybe she should have asked before that. Devlin Russell. She should remember that. He'd think it odd if she didn't.

She knew her responses hadn't been what he'd expected. She could see that much in his eyes. She tried to remember how she should act. How she would have reacted a year or two ago. But that time seemed centuries ago. It was hard to stretch her memory back that far. She abandoned the effort.

She caught Devlin's eyes on her and dipped into the cereal, spooning up a mouthful and swallowing it without tasting it. He'd been kind to her. The thought penetrated the haze of confusion that seemed to surround her these days.

He'd pulled her out of a river, he'd said. That had been kind of him. He couldn't have known that it really didn't matter one way or another. There was no one to care, no one to mourn her death. Least of all her.

There'd been times when she'd thought it would be nice if the haze simply deepened and darkened, sucking her into its depths, swallowing her forever. He'd said she might have jumped into the river.

She frowned down at the cooling cereal, trying to remember the night before. But she couldn't remember anything clearly beyond her car dying. And then there'd been the rain. Or had it been more than rain? Did she remember being in the water? A strong arm snatching her up into the air?

She shook her head. She was tangling memories with imagination. She didn't remember falling into the river. Or jumping? No. She didn't think she'd jumped. If she'd wanted to take that way out, she could have done it a long time ago. It wasn't a fear of death that had stopped her. It was just a feeling that killing herself would hardly be worth the effort. She was all but dead anyway.

Wasn't she?

Devlin watched the faint expressions chase across her face, but he couldn't read anything from them. At least they proved she wasn't an android. He'd begun to wonder, half expecting her to turn down the cereal in favor of a lube and an oil change.

He shook his head at the absurdity of the thought. Maybe he'd been spending too much time alone lately. Maybe he'd just forgotten what the rest of the world was like. But he didn't think Annalise's reactions were normal, no matter how long he'd been away from the real world.

She seemed to sense him watching her. She looked up, a faint frown creasing her wide forehead. Devlin waited for her to speak, but she returned her attention to the cereal without saying anything.

As soon as she was done eating, he'd ask her what she wanted to do, where she wanted to go. If she didn't know, then he'd call Ben Masters and let him come deal with the problem.

But somehow, once she was done eating, he found himself providing her with an old shirt of his and a pair of sweatpants to put on. She accepted the clothes with the same polite thank-you she'd offered for his saving her life. One seemed to mean just as much as the other to her.

And then, he really did want to get started on the shingles. There was no rush to call Ben. He certainly wouldn't be able to dash out right away. It would probably be better to wait until lunchtime anyway.

Maybe all Annalise needed was a little time. Maybe she was still feeling the effects from her fall into the river, though she didn't even seem to remember it. A few hours one way or another wouldn't make any difference.

Devlin kept an eye on her from his perch on the ladder. Certainly no host could complain about her being an overly demanding guest, he thought with a half smile. She'd put on the clothes he gave her and settled herself on the half-finished front porch. She'd been there for two hours now, and as near as he could tell, she hadn't moved in all that time.

She hadn't questioned his allowing her to stay. There wasn't any arrogance about her acceptance of his hospitality. If he'd told her to leave, he was sure she'd have accepted that with the same indifference. She just didn't care where she was.

She sat in the lawn chair that constituted his full supply of outdoor furniture, her hands in her lap, her feet neatly together, and stared at nothing in particular. For a while, it had been interesting to try to guess how long it would be before she moved. But for the past hour, he'd found himself watching to see if she was still breathing.

Depression, Ben had suggested. Comatose seemed like a better description. Devlin set a shingle in place and steadied a nail for the hammer blow. Out of the corner of his eye, he could see Annalise, still as a statue. Was it possible for someone to sit down and simply go into a coma?

Distracted by the thought, he brought the hammer down, missing the nail by an inch and his thumb by a much less comfortable margin. Startled, he released the nail, and both it and the shingle dropped past the ladder to join the debris on the ground.

The curse he muttered was succinct and obscene. He glared at Annalise. She couldn't just sit there. That was all there was to it.

She didn't stir as he climbed down the ladder. It wasn't until he stopped on the porch directly in front of her that she seemed to become aware of his presence. She blinked slowly and tilted her head to look up at him.

"Can you do me a favor?"

The question seemed to confuse her. He didn't know if it was because she didn't understand him or because she couldn't imagine what favor she could do him.

"A favor." It was more a flat repetition than an agreement, but Devlin took it as such. Maybe if she had a reason to do something, she'd come out of that damned shell a little.

"I'm expecting something in the mail," he lied without hesitation. "Could you walk down to the end of the road and see if it's here yet?"

She blinked at him again, her eyes going from his face to the smooth dirt road that stretched out behind him.

"I'd appreciate it," he said, in case she was thinking of refusing. In truth, he doubted she was thinking anything at all.

After a moment, she nodded. It took a moment more for her to stand up and move uncertainly off the porch. She seemed slightly confused to find herself doing something more than staring into space.

Devlin frowned, wondering if he should have left her alone. He probably should have called Ben first thing this morning. It was obvious she had real problems. Maybe a hospital would be the best place for her, someplace where people understood what she was thinking, what she was feeling. But he couldn't quite separate hospital and prison in his mind. And the last thing he wanted was to be a part of anyone being committed—institutionalized.

It wasn't as if he'd sent her on a walk across the continent, he reminded himself. From the ladder, he could see the half mile to the end of the road, so he could keep an eye on her. And since he didn't know of any dangerous animals lurking in the fields of Indiana, the worst that was likely to happen to her was that she'd have a walk on a beautiful spring day.

Part of Annalise was aware of the beauty around her. Sunshine poured down on the empty fields, a warm golden shower that bathed everything in sight. She could feel the same sunshine on her shoulders, warming her face. But the warmth couldn't penetrate to the chill she carried deep inside.

When she'd locked away the part of her that felt pain, she seemed to have slammed the door on every other feeling. She sighed, scuffing her bare feet over the surface of the road, which was still damp from last night's rain.

She'd seen the way Devlin Russell looked at her, sensed the puzzlement in his eyes. She couldn't blame him. Sometimes she felt a sort of puzzlement herself. She could remember another Annalise, someone who'd laughed much more than she cried, someone who'd thrown her arms open to life.

She shook her head, pushing the memories away. That Annalise was gone. It was like remembering someone she'd known a long time ago. It was safer not to remember, not to feel.

The mailbox was empty. Annalise stared at it for a moment before slowly closing the door. She pushed her hands into the pockets of the baggy sweatpants and looked up and down the empty road. Should she wait for the mail carrier or go back to the house?

Before she could make a decision, a rustling in the tall grass beside the mailbox drew her attention. It seemed more than the light breeze could account for. She would have ignored the movement, as indifferent to it as she was to virtually everything else around her, but some small sound accompanied it. Not quite a whimper, nothing as demanding as a cry, it held a plaintive note that pierced straight to feelings Annalise had thought all but dead.

She moved closer and crouched down, peering into the growth of weeds and grasses. It was impossible to see anything, nevertheless she knew the sound hadn't been a product of her imagination. She held out her hand, rubbing her fingers together coaxingly.

"Hello in there," she whispered. She scooted closer. "Who are you?"

There was silence and then a scratchy mew of inquiry.

"A cat, huh?" She rubbed her fingers together again. "Why don't you come out and let me take a look at you?"

Another silence answered her. She waited patiently, aware that her heart was beating much too fast. She was prepared to kneel beside the road all day, if necessary. She hadn't thought she had it in her to care about anything anymore, but she could no more have walked away from the animal than she could have flapped her arms and taken flight.

Another hesitant inquiry, a little louder this time, gave Annalise new hope. The grass stirred, and a pair of golden eyes peered unblinkingly out at her. There was something in that gaze, an almost human wariness that brought a tightness to her chest, as if a fist were squeezing at her heart. Or perhaps as if a terrible pressure were suddenly being eased.

"Come here, kitty. I won't hurt you. Are you all alone out here?" She kept her hand extended and continued the soft patter.

It seemed terribly important that the cat come to her. She couldn't have said quite why. Maybe something in that lonely little cry, in the need that underlay the animal's suspicious gaze, had spoken to some part of her that she'd thought numb forever.

She'd felt a tiny crack in that wall this morning when she'd looked into Devlin Russell's eyes. He'd provided her with food, clothing and saved her life, even if she didn't recall that. He'd asked few questions, made no demands.

The cat crept a few inches closer and Annalise felt the crack widen. She'd never been proof against someone else's need, whether that someone was human or animal. It was one of the things Bill had said he loved about her and part of what had eventually destroyed their marriage.

But she didn't want to think about Bill right now. He was part of another life, part of the hurt she'd tried so hard to lock away. Right now, she was only concerned with the cat, with convincing it to trust her. Maybe she could help the cat even though she'd failed so miserably at helping herself.

Devlin looked over his shoulder and saw Annalise walking back up the driveway. She'd been gone so long, he'd begun to wonder if she'd just kept walking. He'd told himself that it was fine with him if she didn't come back—it would certainly eliminate the problem of what to do with her. But he couldn't deny the relief he felt when he saw her slight figure returning.

Maybe it was the fact that he'd saved her life; maybe it was just that she seemed so helplessly inadequate when it came to taking care of herself—whatever it was, he seemed to feel responsible for her. He didn't *want* to feel that way, but he didn't appear to have much choice in the matter.

Devlin drove a nail into a shingle and turned to look at her again. Her arms appeared to be crossed in front of her body. Her head was bent downward over them. He frowned. Had she injured herself? Fallen maybe?

He slid the hammer through a loop on his leather tool belt and started down the ladder. He was going to feel guilty as hell if he'd sent her off to get the mail he'd known wasn't there and she'd managed to hurt herself.

Devlin reached the ground at the same time that Annalise entered the yard. He started toward her, his quick, urgent strides slowing when he saw that she was uninjured.

Instead of clutching the hideously bleeding wound of his imagination, she was holding a cat. Devlin stopped, letting her cover the remaining distance between them.

Annalise stopped in front of him, lifting her eyes from the cat to meet his. Devlin felt the impact of that look like a blow to the solar plexus. This wasn't the blank stare he'd seen all morning. Her eyes were dark with concern.

"She was down by the mailbox," she said.

"She?" He had to drag his eyes from hers. He stared at the unprepossessing lump of scruffy gray fur in her arms. So she had beautiful eyes. So what. They were just eyes. Blue-green and deep as the ocean, but they were still merely eyes.

"I couldn't simply leave her there," Annalise said, her voice uncertain. "I'm sure she's hungry."

Devlin forced his attention to the cat, who was regarding him with deep suspicion from the safe harbor of Annalise's arms.

"I've got some tuna," he offered, holding out his hand to allow the cat to sniff his fingers. "She's pregnant."

"I know. Do you think someone abandoned her because of that?"

"Probably."

Distress flared in her eyes. Devlin lowered his hand, clenching his fingers against the urge to smooth the frown from her forehead. He'd thought nothing could be more disturbing than the blank lack of expression she'd worn since waking. But he was discovering that Annalise St. John was infinitely more disturbing with life in those wide-set eyes.

Annalise followed him into the house, her attention all for the cat. Devlin opened a can of tuna and emptied it onto a saucer that he set on the kitchen floor. Aside from the obvious bulge of her stomach, the cat was hardly more than skin and bones, but when Annalise lowered her on the floor, she didn't immediately rush toward the food.

She stayed just where she was, her thin body stiff, her eyes wary. She eyed Devlin, weighing the potential hazard he represented. Obligingly he moved back from the food. She hesitated a moment longer and then slinked slowly across the floor. She sniffed at the tuna and then lifted her head to give the surroundings one last careful look before she finally took a bite.

"How long do you think it's been since she last ate?" Annalise asked softly.

Devlin shrugged. "A few days, probably. She's not in bad shape, aside from being a little scrawny."

"How could someone just abandon her like that? When she needed help?"

Devlin looked at her, wondering who had abandoned her when she needed help. Her interest was focused on the cat, who was devouring the tuna with dainty greed.

"They probably told themselves that she'd hunt her own food. People like to believe that lie, especially about cats."

Annalise lifted her eyes from the cat, catching him by surprise as her gaze met his. "Do you mind that I brought her here? I should have asked."

"I don't mind." With those big eyes looking at him uncertainly, he'd probably have said he didn't mind if she wanted to pull his fingernails out.

"I've got to get back to work," he said abruptly, dragging his gaze from hers. What he really needed was some fresh air to blow away the unwelcome realization that Annalise St. John just might be a very attractive woman.

Chapter 4

Annalise spent what remained of the morning and most of the afternoon fussing over the cat. Devlin spent the same period of time trying not to watch Annalise.

It wasn't easy.

There was something remarkably appealing about the picture she and the cat made. Both of them needed more meat on their bones. Both of them had a certain bruised look, as if life had battered them a little too often. Not that it mattered to him what treatment life had handed out to either the woman or the cat.

Devlin tightened his jaw and focused doggedly on the task at hand. Up until today, he'd had no trouble concentrating on whatever needed doing on the house. In fact, he'd enjoyed the vast majority of the work, no matter how repetitive some of it was. It felt good to be building something with his own hands, something strong and enduring.

But when Annalise had tumbled into the river, she'd also tumbled right into the middle of his life. It should have been easy to ignore her. It wasn't as if she demanded attention or chattered his ear off. In fact, she was so quiet, he should have been able to forget her presence completely.

It didn't seem to work that way, however. Thoughts of his houseguest occupied more of his time than Devlin wanted to admit. He kept telling himself that he was going to ask her where she wanted to go—make it clear that he didn't mind fishing her out of the river, but that didn't make her a permanent part of his life.

He could take her into Remembrance and find her a place to stay. Or maybe she'd want to go to the hospital. Just because she was showing signs of life didn't mean all her problems were solved. She might actually welcome a chance to get some medical help.

Somehow, lunch came and went and the afternoon slowly drifted by, and he still hadn't said anything to her about leaving. He told himself that he didn't want to do anything that might turn her back into the unresponsive lump she'd been before finding the cat.

The truth was, she intrigued him. She'd responded with total indifference to the idea that she might have tried to commit suicide, yet she'd nearly cried over the plight of an abandoned animal. She hadn't bothered to wash her face or brush her hair, but she'd carefully bathed the cat with a warm washcloth and spent hours combing knots out of the animal's knotted fur.

Maybe he missed humanity more than he was willing to admit. When he'd left prison, he'd wanted nothing more than to be alone. After so many years spent in forced proximity with hundreds of other men, the very idea that he didn't have to see or hear anyone else for days on end had been paradise.

He'd been content with the way he'd arranged his life. He was close enough to Remembrance to see his sister and his young nephew, the only people he had any interest in. Yet he was away from the hustle and bustle, stuck out in the country, where he might not see anyone but the mail carrier for weeks at a time.

Now, suddenly, Annalise had been dropped into his life, and he was finding that he wasn't as eager to see the last of her as he'd have liked.

Devlin let the day drift by without saying anything about finding her another place to stay. It didn't seem to occur to Annalise to worry about it. If it was someone else, he might have thought she was assuming a bit much, but he didn't think Annalise was being presumptuous.

He didn't think she'd given any thought to the matter at all. From the looks of her, he suspected it had been a long time since she'd thought much about the little details of life, like where she was going to spend the night or where the next meal might be coming from. Especially the meal part of it.

For someone who looked as if they hadn't had a solid meal in weeks, Annalise showed little interest in food. She'd eaten less than half of the roast beef sandwich he'd put in front of her at lunch. She'd fed the rest of its contents to the cat, who showed no hesitation at all about making up for lost dinners.

The sun was starting to sink as Devlin put away the ladder and his tools. It was too late to do anything about settling Annalise somewhere else. She'd have to spend the night. But tomorrow, first thing, he'd tell her that other arrangements had to be made.

When he entered the kitchen, Annalise was sitting on the floor next to the cat, who was polishing off a saucer of tuna. As far as Devlin could tell, the animal had done nothing but eat since her arrival in his home. It didn't seem possible that such a small animal could hold so much food.

Annalise climbed to her feet as he walked to the sink and started to scrub the day's dirt from his hands.

"I hope you don't mind that I opened another can of tuna. Beauty was hungry."

"Beauty?" Devlin gave the scruffy cat a doubting look. True, fed and bathed and combed, she looked considerably better than she had when she first arrived, but the word *beauty* was hardly the first thing that sprang to mind when he saw her.

"She needed a name," Annalise said. "I thought it suited her."

"She's welcome to all the tuna she wants." Devlin answered the original question and sidestepped the necessity for comment on the name.

"Thank you." Annalise watched him work soap into his hands and forearms. He had strong hands, widely palmed with long, blunt fingers. The kind of hands that made you feel safe and protected.

She looked away, focusing on Beauty, who'd finished her meal and had settled down to take a thorough bath. Watching the little cat earnestly cleaning her dull fur, Annalise was suddenly aware of what her hair must look like. She hadn't bothered to comb it, hadn't even looked in a mirror.

How long had it been since she'd cared enough about her appearance to look in a mirror? Weeks? Months, perhaps? She reached up to pat her fingers over her hair. Glancing at Devlin, she saw that he was watching her as he dried his hands. What did he see when he looked at her? A pale, unkempt woman who was too thin, she answered herself promptly.

"I must look pretty awful," she murmured.

"I've seen worse." One corner of his mouth kicked up in a half smile. "You're welcome to use the shower and a comb if you'd like."

"Thank you." Annalise smoothed her hands over the baggy sweatpants, aware that they weren't quite steady. "You've done a great deal for me."

"Not that much." He shrugged. "I've been down on my luck a time or two myself. I ran your clothes through the washer and dryer. They're on the foot of the bed."

"Thank you." She felt as if there should be something more to say, but she couldn't find the words.

"Dinner's in an hour," Devlin said, making it clear that, as far as he was concerned, the conversation was closed.

Annalise took the hint. She wasn't sure what exactly she'd wanted to say anyway.

The bathroom was huge, with a tub the size of a small swimming pool and a separate shower stall. This room seemed the most complete of any she'd seen in the house. Ivory tile covered the shower, as well as surrounding the tub. The walls that weren't tile were painted a matching shade of ivory.

The floor was also tile, a slightly darker shade of gray. The faucets and towel racks were all brass, the golden gleam a warm contrast to the pale ivory. The towels, the bath mat and the fixtures were all a stark black. It was a striking combination. Rather stark but not cold.

Annalise showered, lathering the heavy length of her hair several times. She tried to remember the last time she'd had access to a shower and all the hot water she could stand. The last time she'd been able to afford a motel room, she thought. That had been weeks ago. She'd had that part-time job stocking shelves in a supermarket. Where had that been? Chicago?

She wasn't sure. She'd drifted in and out of so many different places this past year. Ever since— No. It didn't matter since when. She wasn't going to think about that. Not now. Not when she felt a lightening of the misty fog that had all but smothered her these past few months.

When she was at last satisfied that her hair was clean, she shut off the shower and stepped out onto the bath mat. She wrapped her hair in one thick ebony towel and wrapped another sarong-style over her breasts.

She felt warm. The hot shower accounted for only part of that feeling. This was a warmth that was more than skin-deep. Somewhere inside, a thawing had begun. The chill that had gripped her soul for the past year had eased its hold.

Maybe it was Devlin's kindness; maybe it was his asking if she might have jumped into the river the day before. Certainly the thaw owed something to feeling Beauty's small furry body in her arms, to knowing that someone or something needed her.

Annalise stared into the mirror, really looking at herself for the first time in months. She almost regretted her bravery. The mirror reflected her image back to her with merciless clarity. There was no softening of the too-prominent angles of her cheekbones, nothing to add color to her pale skin.

She looked older than she was. She was twenty-five, but she could have passed for ten years older. It wasn't anything as obvious as wrinkles that added years to her age. It was a certain worn look about her skin and the emptiness in her eyes. They looked as empty as her arms felt.

She pushed the thought away and turned from the mirror. What difference did it make how she looked? There was no one to care, no one to even notice.

Devlin was finishing up dinner when Annalise entered the kitchen. He shot her a quick glance as he slid two steaks under the broiler. It took a conscious effort to drag his eyes away. Cleaned up and with a spark of life in her eyes, she was dangerously close to beautiful.

He slammed the broiler door shut. She was still much too thin, of course. The white dress she'd been wearing when she tumbled into the river was too large. It wasn't a particularly attractive dress to begin with. A loose bodice attached to a full skirt that drooped at the waist. It looked old and worn.

But it couldn't detract from the startling improvement in Annalise's appearance. She'd washed her hair and toweled it nearly dry before combing it out. Last night he'd wondered what color it would be when it was dry. Today, he'd noticed little more than that it was lighter than he'd expected. Now he could see that it was a sort of ash blond. It hung thick and straight almost to her waist. It was the kind of hair a man could lose himself in, the kind that was made to be spread over a pillow.

"Is there anything I can do to help?" The question made Devlin realize that he'd been staring at her.

"You can finish setting the table." His tone was abrupt, made more so by the realization that it wasn't as hard as he would have liked to picture Annalise's hair spread across a pillow—his pillow specifically.

They worked in silence broken only by Devlin pointing out the location of plates and silverware. The last of the sunlight disappeared just as they were sitting down to eat. The kitchen was an oasis of light, tucked between the twilight outside and the rest of the house, which was all in darkness.

Devlin cut off a slice of steak and put it into his mouth, chewing slowly. He didn't think he'd ever be able to take good food for granted. A year on the outside and he was still deriving enormous pleasure from something as simple as a well-cooked steak.

"It's very good." Annalise's comment drew his attention to her. "Thank you," she added shyly.

"You're welcome."

She took a few small bites and set her fork down.

"I don't think I thanked you for getting me out of the river," she said slowly.

"You thanked me. Don't let your dinner get cold."

She picked up her fork and ate a little more, but he didn't need to be a mind reader to know her thoughts weren't on her meal.

"I didn't jump," she said abruptly. He shot her a quick glance, but she wasn't looking at him. There didn't seem to be much he could say in reply, so he said nothing, letting her work out her thoughts.

"At least, I don't think I did," she added, as if she felt she should be scrupulously honest.

"You don't owe me any explanations."

"Don't I?" She eyed him uncertainly. "It seems to me that you ought to know, one way or another. The thing is, I'm not a hundred percent certain myself." She toyed with her fork. "I wish I were," she said, her voice hardly more than a whisper.

He was just going to let the subject drop, Devlin thought. He didn't want to get into an emotionally loaded conversation. Whether or not she'd tried to kill herself was a matter of almost complete indifference to him.

"Were you thinking about killing yourself?"

The abrupt question seemed to startle her. She looked at him, her eyes uncertain.

"I don't know." The promptness of the answer made it clear that it was no more or less than the truth.

She really didn't know what had been on her mind, in her heart.

"Does it really matter at all that much, one way or the other?"

"I should know, shouldn't I?"

"Why?"

She stared at him, groping for an answer to the simple question. *Of course,* it was important for her to know what had really happened. After all, you couldn't attempt to kill yourself and not know it. Could you? She frowned and looked away from that cool blue gaze. What did he know, anyway?

"It's just important. That's all." Her answer carried a hint of peevishness that almost made Devlin smile.

"Do you want to die, now?"

"No." Her eyes swept to his again.

"Then does it really matter all that much what you did yesterday? Knowing isn't going to change what happened, whether you fell or jumped. And it isn't going to change how you feel now."

"No, but I'd still like to know."

Devlin took his time chewing and swallowing his last bite of steak and then pushed the plate away. Crossing his forearms on the table in front of him, he looked at her, his eyes unreadable.

"That riverbank isn't all that stable at the best of times. In the midst of a heavy rain, it's even more prone to crumble. You were standing close to the edge. In fact, I was just about to call over to you and warn you when you slipped."

Annalise digested this, feeling a burden lift from her shoulders. "Then you don't think I jumped?"

He shrugged. "I think it's pretty likely that the bank crumbled under you."

"Thank you." Her smile was wider this time, a bit uncertain, as if it had been a long time since she'd used it.

Devlin didn't like the odd little pain that smile caused in his chest. "Your dinner's getting cold," he said brusquely.

Annalise picked up her fork, more to be polite, he suspected, than because she was interested in the food. Whatever the reason, it wouldn't hurt her to eat a bit more.

God, listen to him. He was beginning to sound like a mother hen. He'd never thought of himself as a particularly paternal type, but something about Annalise brought out a long-buried urge to fuss. He'd just as soon bury it again, he thought sourly.

"Where do you live?"

Annalise's fork hit the plate with a snap.

"Live?" She repeated the word as if unsure of its meaning.

"I was just wondering if there was someone who'd be worried about you."

He was watching her face carefully and he thought he saw a tinge of relief, as if the second question was easier to answer than the first.

"No, there's no one." She hesitated but seemed to feel the need to add something. "I've been traveling for a while, actually. I don't really have a permanent address."

Or a temporary one, either, he'd be willing to bet. It would have been cruel to ask her why she'd been traveling or what she'd been doing. He might be many things, but cruel was not one of them.

"Do you have a car?" She blinked at him, as if the question was a difficult one.

"Yes," she said slowly, frowning as if the memory were vague. "It died. I didn't know what to do. So far from town and all."

He didn't believe for one minute that she had any idea of how far she was from Remembrance. He doubted she even knew where the nearest town was. But he didn't pursue the question. He neither expected nor wanted her to spill her guts to him. She was welcome to her secrets, whatever they were.

"Oh!" The sudden exclamation brought Devlin's eyes to her.

"What's wrong?"

"It just occurred to me that I haven't even asked you if you'll let me spend the night here again."

The embarrassed color that flooded her cheeks was really rather attractive, he decided. It made her eyes seem darker, wider.

"You're welcome to stay the night."

"You must think I'm a dreadful person." She pushed her half-eaten dinner away, her distress obvious. "I've barely thanked you for saving my life. I hardly even acknowledge your kindness and then I presume on your hospitality. You should have gotten rid of me hours ago."

"Don't worry about it." Devlin ignored the fact that, hours ago, he'd been thinking exactly the same thing. "Everybody needs a little help now and then."

"But I shouldn't have just assumed I could stay here."

"I don't mind." He reached across the table, closing his hand over the fingers she was twisting together. The impact of the small touch was more than he'd expected. Her hands felt so delicate beneath his, as fragile and vulnerable as a child's.

He was torn between conflicting urges. He wanted to put his arms around her and tell her everything would be all right, that he'd keep the world from hurting her again. And he wanted to carry her into the bedroom and see just exactly what that heavy length of hair looked like spread across his pillow.

"You're welcome to stay the night," he said again. He drew his hand away casually. Annalise didn't seem to have noticed anything unusual about the moment.

"I can't offer to pay you," she said with difficulty.

"Good. Because I wouldn't accept it." He pushed back from the table and stacked their plates. He felt her eyes following him as he moved to the counter. After a moment, she stood up and cleared the table of their glasses. Devlin took them from her and placed them in the dishwasher.

"I really do appreciate everything you've done for me," she said.

"I haven't done all that much." He snapped shut the latch on the dishwasher and turned to look back at her. He really wished she didn't look so vulnerable and so uncertain. The protective shell she'd locked herself inside of was breaking up around her.

"Tomorrow, I'll get myself out of your hair," she said.

"We'll worry about it tomorrow." Devlin pretended not to see the uncertainty in her eyes. He knew as well as she did that getting her out of his hair was going to be more than a matter of simply waving goodbye as she disappeared into the sunset.

Hours later, hands beneath his head, Devlin stared up at the ceiling. The exposed beams were nothing more than deeper shadows in the darkness above him. He'd considered, briefly, putting in a ceiling, but he liked the feeling of spaciousness that the open beams gave.

But his thoughts weren't on the architecture. And they weren't on the next day's tasks. Since the day he'd decided to build a home, the house had occupied most of his waking hours, either thinking about it or working on it.

Tonight his thoughts weren't on plaster versus drywall or whether to build a deck or pour a patio. Instead, he was thinking about the woman who now occupied his bed—his comfortable bed, he amended, taking note of just how hard the floor was, even with an air mattress beneath him.

It didn't take a genius to guess that Annalise had hit rock bottom. The emptiness that had been in her eyes this morning had told of someone who no longer cared what became of them. She hadn't reacted when he'd asked her if she'd tried to commit suicide, because it really hadn't mattered to her.

When she awakened to find herself alone with a strange man, she hadn't shown any of the normal concern a woman might have been expected to feel. And he didn't believe it was because he had a particularly winning smile. She hadn't been worried about what he might do to her, because nothing could be worse than whatever she'd already experienced.

What had happened to her to drive her so low? Rape? The thought brought a slow flush of anger to his face. He'd long believed that a man who'd force a woman was something less than human. But the thought that someone might have raped Annalise brought that contempt into focus, sharpened it with a more personal rage.

He forced his tight muscles to relax. He didn't know that that was what had happened to drive all the life from her. Time enough to find the son of a bitch and castrate him if he found out that was the case.

Odd how she'd literally dropped into his life less than twenty-four hours ago, and here he was lying awake wondering about her. He frowned into the darkness. He had the feeling that he should have let Ben take her to the hospital the night before. Already he was getting involved. No matter how tenuous that involvement, it wasn't for him.

But he couldn't just walk away from her. His mouth twisted in rueful acceptance. Like it or not, he cared what happened to Annalise. She'd brought out feelings he'd thought only Kelly could stir in him. Feelings of protectiveness and concern, things he didn't particularly want to feel.

Maybe it was the fact that he'd saved her life. Maybe you couldn't save someone's life without them becoming real to you. Perhaps it was the vulnerability in her eyes. He couldn't ignore that look, the fragility of her. Physically she looked as if a stiff breeze could carry her away. But it was the uncertainty in her eyes that spoke to him.

Finding the cat seemed to have cracked her shell. Beauty. He grinned into the darkness. The name was pure wishful thinking. The cat looked like a scruffy, furry gray basketball. But Annalise had looked at her and called her Beauty. There was something ineffably poignant about that.

Thirty-six hours ago, he'd had nothing more on his mind than what color to paint the window trim. Now he had a woman who needed a lot of careful handling if she wasn't to retreat back into whatever hell she'd been hiding in when he found her; and a cat who looked as if she were about to deliver a litter of fifty any minute and in the meantime was threatening to eat him out of house and home.

Devlin shook his head and closed his eyes. Time enough to worry about both of them in the morning.

He might have been more concerned if he could have seen the half smile that softened his mouth as he drifted off to sleep. He didn't look at all like a man who'd taken on unsolicited burdens.

Chapter 5

When Annalise awoke, the first thing she was aware of was that she didn't feel as if a heavy weight were sitting on her chest, making every breath almost more of an effort than it was worth. She snuggled her head deeper into the pillow, keeping her eyes closed as she took a mental inventory.

She sensed that it was still early, probably not much past dawn. But she didn't feel like going back to sleep. She was awake and she wanted to stay awake. For the first time in months, she felt a sense of anticipation for the coming day.

A small movement alerted her to the fact that she wasn't the bed's only occupant. She opened her eyes, her mouth curving in a soft smile when she saw Beauty stretched out beside her. Annalise stroked her fingers over the little cat's head. Beauty opened her eyes, giv-

ing her an unreadable look before closing them again.
The rumble of her purr made it clear that Annalise's
attentions were acceptable.

Annalise's smile widened. The cat felt full of life,
content with her lot. Of course, her lot was pretty
darned good at the moment. She had tuna for breakfast, lunch and dinner and a comfortable bed to spend
her nights in. Much the same as her own lot, Annalise
thought, her smile fading.

Maybe it was time to look ahead, to try to put some
order into her life. These past few months were little
more than a smoky blur. She'd probably never remember all the places she'd been. But as Devlin had
said, the past was past. She couldn't go back and
change things. She could only move on from here.

Devlin. She'd known him only a day and still knew
virtually nothing about him; yet she had the feeling
that she knew him well. Something deep inside her responded to him, telling her this was a man she could
trust, not just with her life, which he'd already saved,
but with her soul.

Odd, for the past year, she hadn't been entirely sure
she still had a soul. She'd more than half believed it
had died when she'd lost the only person in the world
who meant anything to her. But it seemed it had just
retreated away from the black pain that had gripped
her for so long.

She scratched under Beauty's chin. Maybe what
she'd needed all along was for someone or something
to need her again. Or maybe, she'd had to go through
a period of mourning before she'd be able to respond
to that need.

When Devlin had asked her if she'd tried to kill herself, he'd chiseled the first small crack in the wall she'd built to protect herself. Life had held little value for a long time, but hearing that it had almost been taken from her, perhaps by her own actions, had struck her harder than she'd realized at the time.

She sat up, dislodging the cat, who gave her a huffy look before jumping from the bed, hitting the floor with a less than dainty thud. Annalise hardly noticed her indignant departure. She swung her legs off the bed and then sat without moving, staring at the bare plywood beneath her feet.

Just where was she going to go from here? It was all very well and good that she was starting to rejoin the living, but that didn't make all her problems go away. She had no money, no place to live, no job and no prospects of getting any of them.

She fought back the depression she could feel hovering in the background, ready to swoop down and swallow her whole. Squaring her shoulders, she stood up.

There'd been a time when her optimism had been so strong it might almost have been considered a character flaw. It might take a long time to recapture that optimism. She might never regain it. But she wasn't going back to the gray emptiness that had characterized her life for so long.

She had a long way to go before she had her life in order. But she could only take it one step at a time and hope to God that there was firm ground to step onto.

Devlin had showered and shaved in the second bathroom and was cooking breakfast when Annalise made an appearance.

"Good morning."

"Hi." Devlin returned his attention to the bacon, trying to ignore the sharp pinch of awareness he felt. Damn, why couldn't I have fished a ninety-year-old lady out of the river?

"Is there anything I can do to help?" In the face of his less-than-enthusiastic greeting, Annalise's smile faded, her eyes taking on the uncertain look that made his chest ache.

"Sure. You can tell me how you like your eggs and then you can butter the toast." Devlin made a conscious effort to soften his voice. It wasn't her fault that she made him think of hot nights and cool sheets.

A few minutes later, they sat down at the kitchen table. Ordinarily Devlin ate at the breakfast bar, but he preferred to have Annalise across the table from him than sitting inches away on a stool.

She had more appetite this morning, he noticed. She was doing justice to the bacon and eggs. He waited until they'd both finished eating before breaking the silence.

"Do you remember where your car is?"

"I think so." She frowned, trying to bring better focus to blurred memories. "It died and I pulled it off the road. I remember seeing an old barn. It looked like it was about to collapse."

Devlin nodded. "I think I know the place. It's a couple of miles from where I first saw you, though. Did you walk far?"

Annalise thought about it for a minute and then shook her head. "I don't know. I . . . wasn't thinking very clearly, I'm afraid."

"Don't worry about it. There aren't all that many dilapidated barns around. Chances are it's the one I'm thinking of." He rose from the table and picked up both their plates. "Why don't we go take a look at your car? If I can't get it running, we'll tow it back here."

Annalise started to protest that he'd already done more than enough for her, but she closed her mouth without speaking. Without a car, she couldn't go anywhere. No doubt, Devlin had already thought of that. He was probably anxious to get her car in running condition and get her out of his hair.

They left the house a few minutes later. Devlin stopped on the porch, frowning down at her bare feet. "You can't keep running around without shoes. With all the construction that's been done on this place, the whole area is probably full of nails and bits of wire and God knows what else."

Annalise curled her toes against the floorboards. "I don't have any shoes."

"No. I suspect they were lost in the river," he said absently, still frowning at her feet. "Hang on."

He disappeared back into the house, leaving Annalise to contemplate the embarrassment of being so completely incompetent in providing for herself that she was dependent on someone else for something as basic as shoes.

Devlin was gone only a minute, returning with a pair of white sneakers in his hand. "Here. See if these come close to fitting."

Annalise took the sneakers from him and sat down on the edge of the steps. A moment later, she stood up, flexing her toes inside the slightly stiff canvas.

"They fit."

"Good. Kelly left them last time she was here. I should have thought of these yesterday before asking you to check the mail."

"Kelly?" Annalise hung back when he stepped off the porch. "Are you sure she won't mind me borrowing her shoes?"

"Positive." Devlin turned back, narrowing his eyes against the bright morning sun. "She'd be glad you could use them."

"Oh." Annalise followed him to his truck, aware that the shoes didn't feel as nice as they had a moment ago. Who was Kelly? A girlfriend, no doubt. The thought caused an odd twinge of something that could have been, but wasn't, dislike.

"She sounds nice," she said as Devlin inserted the key in the ignition.

"Who?" He glanced at her questioningly as he started the truck.

"Kelly. She sounds nice."

"She is. Always has been, actually." He put the truck in gear and started down the driveway.

"So you've known her a long time?" They were probably practically married, she thought. Maybe he was even building the house for the two of them.

"All my life." He shot her a curious look. "She's my sister."

"Your sister?" Annalise felt her mood lighten. Not that it had anything to do with finding out that she was wearing his sister's shoes and not his lover's. "She lives near here?"

"In Remembrance."

He didn't seem interested in expanding on the bare-bones information, and Annalise didn't pursue the topic. She doubted if he'd have told her even that much if she hadn't questioned him.

It didn't take them long to find her car, pulled crookedly off to one side of the road. Annalise felt as if she were seeing the little compact for the first time in months.

The car had been a wedding present from Bill. His family had been wealthy, and by the time they married when she was nineteen and he was twenty-two, he'd already come into two trust funds. Buying a car for a wedding gift had been nothing out of the ordinary for the Stevens family.

She remembered how excited she'd been, examining every inch of shiny blue paint, polishing out imaginary smudges on the bumper with the hem of her shirt. Now the paint had faded to a dirty gray shade and the bumpers were pitted with rust. The little car looked unloved and unkempt. Reflecting its owner, she thought bleakly.

She smoothed her hand over the cheap cotton of her skirt. She hadn't taken any better care of the car this past year than she'd taken of herself. And they'd both suffered some wear and tear as a result.

Devlin pulled his truck in behind the car and got out. After a moment, Annalise followed him. She wasn't at all sure she wanted to get any closer to the car. It held so many memories. She'd gone from happily married to single to destitute in that car. For the past few months, she'd lived in it more often than not, sleeping curled awkwardly across the front seats.

As Annalise reached the rear of the car, Devlin opened the driver's side door and reached in to pull the keys out of the ignition.

"I guess I wasn't too worried about anyone stealing it," she said uneasily, though he hadn't, by so much as a look, commented on her carelessness.

"I guess." The look he ran over the car made it clear that he thought any such worries would have been close to delusional. He slid behind the wheel with some difficulty. The seat was adjusted for legs considerably shorter than his, and his efforts to push it back proved useless.

Annalise linked her hands together in front of her, watching as he cranked the engine without result. A look under the hood didn't produce any miraculous solution. Devlin lowered the hood and pulled a rag out of his back pocket, wiping his hands as he considered the battered little car.

"Is it something awful?" Annalise asked at last.

"I don't know. How long has it been since you had a tune-up done?" Her blank look told him it had been considerably longer than it should have been. "It could just be that it needs points and plugs." He shrugged. "Or it could be one of half a dozen other things."

"Oh." There didn't seem to be much she could add to that single word. She didn't need to tell him that she didn't have the money for a tune-up, let alone the half a dozen other things it might require. He hadn't asked about her financial state, but he had known it was nearly nonexistent.

If Devlin was aware of the blow his words had dealt to her fragile optimism, he didn't show it. He looked up and down the road, frowning in thought.

"There's no sense in trying to do anything with it here. I brought a tow chain. I'll tow it back to my place."

Annalise nibbled on her lower lip. She wanted to ask him to just tow it to the nearest service station and she'd deal with it from there. But the truth was, a service station was going to want money even to look at the car. And money was something she had all too little of.

While Devlin moved the truck around to the front of her car, Annalise opened the passenger door. Her purse was lying on the floor in front of the seat, an open invitation to anyone who'd happened by. On the other hand, the purse wouldn't have been much loss. When Shakespeare wrote that "Who steals my purse steals trash;" he could have been writing for her.

Even the purse itself wasn't worth stealing. It was cheap brown plastic that had started to crack on the corners, an advertisement that its contents were no more valuable than it was.

Perched on the edge of the seat, she opened it, examining its contents as if someone might have dropped a wad of one-hundred dollar bills in when she wasn't looking. But it was the same pathetic inventory she'd been seeing for months: a lipstick she hadn't used in weeks, a checkbook for an account she no longer had, a pocketknife that had gotten damp and rusted shut, a handful of small change and four tattered dollar bills.

Her fingers trembled on the edge of a leather photo wallet, its quality a contrast to its surroundings. She hadn't opened the wallet in almost a year. The images it held were just too painful. Not that she'd noticed the pain growing any less for avoiding the photos.

Suddenly she wanted desperately to open the wallet. What if her memories had grown dim? What if she was no longer remembering clearly? After all, her memories of forty-eight hours ago were blurred. She toyed with the clasp, feeling her pulse speed with something close to fear.

"I've got everything hooked up."

Annalise jumped, her hand jerking back from the wallet as if she'd just been caught shoplifting. She slipped out of the car and faced him, the purse clutched defensively in front of her.

"I was just looking at things."

Devlin lifted one brow in surprise. "They're your things," he said mildly.

"Of course. Of course they are." Annalise forced her fingers to relax their death grip on the cheap plastic purse. He must think she was a total idiot. Not that he could have had much doubt even before this latest demonstration.

"I've got the tow chain hooked up," Devlin said, offering no comment on her odd reaction.

Annalise followed him back to the truck. She had to get herself under control. A tall order when she hadn't managed anything close to that in months.

Devlin was aware of his passenger's tension as he towed the battered compact back to his house. He wasn't quite sure what had triggered it, whether it was seeing the car or something in the ugly purse she clutched with white-knuckled fingers.

From the looks of her car, he'd consider it a miracle if it didn't need everything from the chassis up replaced. And he wouldn't bet much on the condition of the chassis. It was a wonder it had run as long as it had.

So much for getting her off his hands today. But he couldn't pretend to feel the disappointment he wanted to at that thought. The truth was, it had been rather pleasant to go out to the kitchen this morning and see that scruffy cat waiting to be fed. And it had felt good to lean against the counter and watch the sun coming up, cup of coffee in hand, and know that there was someone else in the house, someone else to concern himself with.

If he was honest, he had to admit that maybe Annalise provided the same thing for him that the cat had given her—a chance to be needed. Maybe he was lying to himself in thinking that he could make his life away from the rest of the world, that he didn't miss occasional human contact.

Not that he was particularly anxious to open his doors to the entire world or even to a tiny portion of it on a permanent basis. But it wouldn't be so bad having a houseguest for a while. She'd have time to put her life back together, and he'd get the chance to feel as if he were helping her out.

One thing he'd learned was that there wasn't much personal satisfaction in handing out sums of money to worthy charities. Oh, it helped to soothe his conscience, which still pinched over his accepting the money in the first place.

It didn't matter how logical Reed's arguments had been or how right he was, there was still a part of Devlin that regarded Sampson's fortune as nothing more than the biblical thirty pieces of silver, only he'd somehow sold himself down the river.

But Annalise didn't need his money. Or at least, that wasn't all she needed, he amended, glancing in the rearview mirror of her car. It seemed to him that what she needed, more than money, was time. Time to rest, time to heal.

Who knows, maybe in helping Annalise St. John to heal her wounds, he'd find a way to heal some of his own.

After Devlin maneuvered her dead car into position near the house and unhooked the tow chain, Annalise pulled a cardboard box of clothing out of the narrow back seat. She'd sold her suitcase to a pawnshop months ago—in Saint Louis, she thought.

She set the box on the ground and looked at the remaining items in the car. Everything she owned in the world was in that car. She doubted if all of it, including the car, would bring more than fifty dollars.

She was twenty-five years old, with no marketable skills, emotions that seesawed between optimism and despair and no idea of where she was going to sleep tonight.

No, that wasn't quite true. She hadn't known Devlin long, but it was long enough to be sure that he wasn't going to throw her out in the street. Or in this case, the field. He'd see her settled somewhere. But where?

"There's a washer and dryer in the utility room behind the kitchen. You're welcome to use them." Devlin had come up behind her with that quiet walk she was coming to associate with him. He stood looking over her shoulder at the car's rather meager contents, his expression unreadable.

"I was just thinking that it's not a lot to show for a quarter of a century." She forced lightness into her tone. Devlin's gaze shifted from the car to her.

"I've never thought it was a good idea to measure success by what you have. Possessions are the easiest thing in the world to take away."

"True. So I suppose I'm in a pretty good position since I've got nothing left to lose."

"That's one way of looking at it," he said with a half smile. He glanced down at the box of clothing. "There's soap in the cupboard over the washer. If you need anything else, let me know."

Annalise's eyes followed him as he walked away. She bent down to pick up the box, but her thoughts followed Devlin. Did he ever smile all the way? Something more than that cautious upturn at one corner of his mouth?

It wasn't any of her business if Devlin Russell never smiled again, of course. But something about him suggested a hard-won reserve. As if he'd found that being open was too painful, that caring too often ended in hurting.

"I suppose I'm the last one to tell him different," she said, addressing the remark to Beauty, who'd risen from her corner of the kitchen to follow Annalise into the utility room.

"I'm hardly a walking advertisement for the bene-fits of caring about people." She dumped the clothes into the washer and started the machine. Beauty beat a hasty retreat from the sound of the water. Annalise followed her into the kitchen, bending to pick up the rotund little animal, cradling her against her chest. Beauty immediately began to rumble her approval of this treatment, kneading her paws against Annalise's arm.

Annalise carried the cat with her as she left the kitchen. For the first time since her rather unortho-dox arrival, she really looked at the house, trying to envision it with the walls finished and proper flooring laid down. With furniture and curtains and pictures on the wall.

It had the potential to be a beautiful home. The rooms were big and airy, the windows occupied al-most as much space as the walls, bringing the outside in, making the rooms seem even larger than they were.

Was he building this house for himself? Did he plan to share it with someone? Just because Kelly had turned out to be his sister didn't mean there wasn't a woman in his life, someone who'd had a say in designing the open floor plan, in picking out the tile in the bathroom, the kitchen cupboards.

"I don't think so," she murmured to the cat, whose eyes were nearly closed. There was something about Devlin that spoke of aloofness—an indefinable reserve that made it hard for her to believe that there was a special someone in his life, someone he let down his guard with. Someone who'd seen him really smile.

She sighed and set Beauty down. Whether he smiled and whether he had someone to share this house with were not her concern. Her concern was figuring out where to go from here. One of her foster mothers had once told her that every journey began with the first step—a useful truism. The problem was figuring out in which direction that first step should be.

With the vague idea that taking an inventory of her belongings might bring some inspiration, Annalise went back outside. She'd assumed Devlin was working on the section of the house he'd been shingling the day before. Instead, she found him bent over the engine compartment of her car, wrench in hand. Two spark plugs lay beside him on the fender already.

He looked up as she stopped across the car from him. "Well, the plugs definitely aren't helping things any. And the points are badly burned. The oil is low and it's also filthy. It has to be changed. Your plug wires could use replacing, too. Until I can get it running, it's hard to say what else might be wrong. Maybe a tune-up is all it really needs."

He set a third spark plug beside the other two and reached for the next one. "I've got some things I need to pick up in town this afternoon. I'll get the parts while I'm there."

"You can't!" The worlds came out more forcefully than she'd intended. Devlin straightened away from the car, resting his greasy hands on the fender as he looked at her.

"If you're worried about the money, forget it."

"I can't forget it. You've already done so much for me."

"I haven't done that much, and the cost of a few parts isn't going to cause me any problems."

"That's not the point," she insisted, her voice nearly strangled with embarrassment. "I can't just keep on taking and taking from you. You saved my life. You've taken care of me. You don't even know me."

"Look, we went over this before. You thanked me for saving your life. And as far as taking care of you goes, I haven't done anything incredible. A place to sleep and a little food aren't going to get me nominated for sainthood."

Annalise twisted her hands together in front of her, struggling for the words to make him see how she felt. All her life, she'd always taken her fair share of any work that was to be done. Her parents had been killed in a car wreck when she was eight and she'd been put in foster care. One thing she'd quickly learned was that it made her life easier if she did her best not to be a burden to anyone.

It was a lesson that had carried on into her adult life. She'd continue to work after she and Bill were married, not because they needed the money but because she had to know that she was pulling her own weight, even if it was in low-end secretarial jobs that didn't pay that much.

Bill had laughed and said he didn't care what she did as long as she as happy. But she didn't think Bill had ever understood just why she needed her "little job," as he'd called it. If Bill hadn't been able to understand, even when he'd loved her, how was she supposed to make Devlin understand?

But Devlin did understand. More than she could have imagined. The need to be beholden to no one was something he understood very well. From early childhood on, he'd known what it was to have only himself to depend on. His father had been abusive. His mother had simply retreated into another world where unpleasant things didn't happen, and Devlin had learned to survive without depending on either of them.

"I wasn't going to mention this yet, but it looks like now is as good a time as any." He tossed the greasy rag down and leaned one hip against the front of the car, crossing his arms over his chest and fixing her with a cool blue gaze.

"Mention what?" He was probably going to tell her that he'd really hoped to get her out of his hair by now or that her car positively needed a complete overhaul. She dropped her hands to her sides, concealing their trembling in the folds of her skirt.

"How are you at organizing?"

"Organizing?" The question was so far from what she'd been expecting that he might have been speaking a foreign language.

"And dealing with people on the phone?"

"I...I used to do secretarial work," she said slowly. "And I worked as a receptionist for six months."

Devlin nodded thoughtfully. "Sounds good."

"Good for what?" She hardly dared to hope that it might be what it sounded like. If he knew of a job...

"Are you interested in going to work?"

"Yes." She gripped the folds of her skirt, trying to contain the hope that was welling up inside. Just because he knew of a possible job, it didn't mean she'd be qualified for it. After all, she hadn't worked steadily in almost three years. And it wasn't as if her qualifications had been stunning before that.

"Good. I need someone to deal with suppliers for me and to organize the paperwork on building the house. I've been throwing everything in a drawer. I can offer you room and board and a reasonable salary."

The figure he named seemed more than reasonable, when you added in room and board. Annalise swallowed the urge to shout an acceptance.

"You don't have to invent a job for me," she told him, her chin lifting in an unconscious gesture of pride. "If there's something I can help you with, I'd be happy to do it. There's no need to pay me."

"Not very practical of you," he commented, arching one brow. "Besides, I always believe in paying someone who works for me."

"But you've already done so much for me," she protested.

"We've already talked about that." He waved one hand to dismiss the issue. "I could use someone to handle the paperwork and the suppliers. Do you think you could do it?"

"Yes." She nodded slowly. The kind of work he was describing wasn't difficult, and it was similar to jobs she'd held in the past.

"But you don't have to pay me for it. Room and board would be more than enough."

"The salary goes with it," he said flatly. "That's my offer, take it or leave it."

Annalise stared at him, wondering how it was possible to feel so much gratitude toward someone and, at the same time, have the urge to smack them. He knew she didn't have a real choice. What else could she do? It occurred to her to wonder if she was crazy to be upset with him for being *too* generous.

"All right," she said at last. "But don't think I'm not going to earn my keep."

"I wouldn't think that." Though his expression was solemn, Annalise could see the smile in his eyes. He held out his hand and she put her own into it. His fingers closed over hers, warm and strong.

Annalise smiled, hoping he couldn't feel the way her pulse had accelerated. Nerves, she told herself. It was just nerves.

Chapter 6

When Devlin got back from town that afternoon, he had not only car parts and the nails he'd needed for the shingling, but also a new bed and a small chest of drawers.

Annalise had started out with great plans to begin work immediately on the rather large box of papers he'd handed her before he left, but sometime around one o'clock, she'd found herself nodding off at the table. She'd settled onto the sofa to rest just for a moment and didn't wake until Devlin pushed open the front door two hours later.

Startled, she jerked upright, staring at him dazedly as he carried a mattress through the living room and into one of the unfinished rooms off it. He passed by her again, nodding to her as he disappeared out the door.

Annalise pushed her hair off her face, trying to shake off the thickheaded feeling that was an inevitable result of sleeping in the middle of the day. She had only partially succeeded when Devlin entered the house again, this time with a box spring balanced on his back.

She cleared her throat as he reappeared. "What was that?"

"A bed," he said, and disappeared out the front door.

Annalise blinked. A bed. Of course. Why hadn't that occurred to her? She'd thought it might be a rhinoceros.

This time, when he came back in carrying pieces of a bed frame, she followed him. He put the pieces on the floor and pulled a screwdriver out of his pocket before kneeling down to begin assembling the frame.

"What are you doing?"

He shot her a look that said he was beginning to have doubts about her intelligence. "I'm putting together a bed frame."

"I know that. *Why* are you doing it?"

"Because it won't hold the box spring and mattress unless it's put together."

He was being deliberately obtuse. She knew it and he knew it. He was hoping she'd drop the subject and the argument he sensed she was going to offer.

"Did you buy this bed for me?" Obviously the only way she was going to get a real answer was to ask the real question.

"Generally, when you're offered room and board, the room includes a bed," he said without looking up from the task at hand.

"I could have slept on the sofa," she protested, distressed that he'd spent money on her.

"No, you couldn't."

"Then, you can take the cost of the bed out of my salary."

"No."

The blunt refusal silenced her momentarily. She stared at him, searching for something to say. When the silence stretched, Devlin looked up. Seeing the distress in her face, he put down the screwdriver and stood up.

"Look, don't make a bigger deal out of this than it is. I'd planned on this being a spare bedroom," he lied without hesitation. In truth, he'd been thinking of putting exercise equipment in this room. "It can't be a spare bedroom without a bed. I just bought the bed a little sooner, that's all."

"It seems like I've already taken so much from you," she said unhappily.

"Like what? You don't eat as much as that cat. Besides a few ounces of food, what have I given you?"

"It's not material things I'm talking about."

"Well, the bed is very material and I'm not taking it back and you're not sleeping on the sofa. I'm going to put this together and then you can sleep standing up in the closet if you'd prefer."

Annalise recognized defeat. "At least, let me cook dinner."

"Can you cook?"

"Yes."

"Then the kitchen is all yours."

It wasn't until she went to bed that she realized that a bed wasn't the only thing Devlin had bought. A small chest of drawers sat against one wall and a thick throw rug had been placed next to the bed so that her feet wouldn't encounter the wooden subfloor first thing in the morning.

There was a set of sheets and two pillows placed neatly in the middle of the new mattress. And not just plain white sheets, either, she saw when she opened them. They were off-white with a delicate sprinkling of lavender flowers scattered over them. There was a night table and a simple porcelain lamp beside the bed.

The small bathroom that opened off the room had been stocked with soap, shampoo and towels. There was even a bottle of bubble bath sitting on the edge of the tub.

Annalise picked the bottle up and opened it, inhaling the light floral scent. She put the lid back on, feeling tears sting the backs of her eyes. It was too much. The job, buying parts for her car, furnishing a room for her, buying her bubble bath. He'd just done too much.

She knew better than to argue with him anymore, though. It wouldn't get her anywhere. He could hardly return the bubble bath, anyway. She was just going to have to make sure she proved worthy of the efforts he'd gone to. She didn't want him to ever have cause to regret all he'd done for her.

She bent to turn on the taps, adjusting the water to something just short of scalding. It had been a long time since she'd had a chance to soak in a luxuriously full tub.

Sprawled in a big leather recliner in the master bedroom, Devlin heard the hum in the pipes as Annalise turned the water on. He was aware of an almost imperceptible easing of tension. He'd more than half expected her to protest when she saw that there was more than a bed in the room.

Actually, a bed was all he'd planned to buy, but it had occurred to him that she could hardly keep her clothes in that pathetic cardboard box. As an inveterate reader, he considered a lamp by the bed to be essential, which meant he had to get a table to put it on.

The bed required sheets, and while he was buying sheets, he'd realized that the bathroom had no towels. From there, it had been an easy step to soap and shampoo.

He leaned his head back, his book forgotten. He couldn't quite remember when he'd enjoyed shopping as much as he had this afternoon. Not that he hadn't derived a definite satisfaction in choosing the things that had gone into the house right from the start. But it hadn't been quite the same.

He'd found himself wondering what Annalise's taste was like. Would she prefer a floral design on her sheets or did she like the sharp edges of geometrics? What colors did she like?

He heard her shut the water off. She'd be stepping into the tub now. She'd probably pinned her hair up on top of her head, but there'd be a few tendrils that managed to escape. The bathroom would be slightly steamy, lending a soft-focus look to her pale skin.

He closed his eyes, wishing he didn't know quite so clearly what she looked like without her clothes. Odd, how when he'd had her naked in the shower with him, he'd felt not the slightest trace of sexual awareness. His only concern had been to get her warm, and he'd thought he noticed little more than that she was too thin.

But suddenly, he was remembering other things. Like the softness of her breasts pressed against his arm, the sleek length of her legs, the intriguing triangle of curls at the top of her thighs.

He shifted uncomfortably in the chair, his eyes snapping open. His jeans were suddenly too tight. With a groan, he stood up, dropping the book onto the bed as he strode to the window.

He was acting like a randy teenager, getting hard just because a woman happened to be taking a bath a couple of rooms away. He'd had eight years to conquer his random sexual urges, eight years to contemplate the high cost of his carelessness about whom he slept with.

And in the year since leaving prison, he'd managed to maintain that iron control. Sexual release wasn't worth the potential price it extracted. He'd channeled everything he had into building this house, into purging himself of eight years of hell.

It wasn't as if he hadn't seen women he found attractive this past year. He'd contemplated the advantages of establishing a pleasant, no-strings-attached relationship with some mature woman, based on little more than satisfying a mutual physical need.

But he hadn't quite figured out how to go about establishing such a relationship—he could hardly take out an ad. Besides, sooner or later, most women wanted something more. They generally craved the kind of emotional ties he could never give.

So he'd clamped the lid on his sexual needs. He hadn't found it all that difficult. Until now. Maybe it was the vulnerability in Annalise's eyes or the way she nibbled on her lower lip when she was thinking. Or maybe it was the fragile build of her that made him want to see if his hands could span her waist or just how neatly her breast would fit his palm.

He wanted to see her wearing nothing but that extravagant length of hair draped over her body. He wanted to wind his fingers in it and pull her close. He wanted to feel her mouth parting under his and her thighs opening to accept him into her.

"Damn!" The word was a groan. Devlin spun away from the window, forcing the images from his mind. He had to think of something else. Like whether or not he had enough shingles to finish the house or what color to paint the living room.

Or the soft glow of Annalise's skin as she stepped from the bath.

Growling a low, frustrated curse, he strode from the bedroom, turning toward the back door. Once outside, he drew in a deep lungful of cool night air. A brisk walk. That was what he needed. A nice brisk walk. In ten or twelve miles he'd have managed to forget all about the woman he'd just asked to live in his house for an indefinite period of time.

Annalise awoke to discover she was sharing her pillow with a purring cat. Seeing that she was awake, Beauty stood up, chirped a greeting and jumped off the bed, hitting the floor with a thump. The sound made Annalise smile. So much for the silent slink of the cat. Of course, Beauty was at a bit of a disadvantage at the moment. It was probably pretty hard to slink with a belly the size of hers.

Her smile faded, one hand creeping to her flat stomach. She snatched her fingers away, forcing her thoughts to focus solely on the coming day. Today she was going to get started on proving to Devlin that she was something more than a charity case. He'd hired her to organize his records and deal with suppliers, and that was just what she was going to do.

It was the most content day Annalise had spent in months. Not only did she have a roof over her head and a job, she felt as if she were getting herself back. She was starting to recover the determined optimism that had kept her going through assorted foster homes and life's assorted curves.

She'd fallen about as low as it was possible to get this past year, but she wasn't going to dwell on the past. Neither was she quite ready to look too far into the future. But she could focus on each day as it came, which was a step up from where she'd been for so long, when one day had meant nothing more or less than the last.

She spent the morning sorting receipts into neat little piles on the breakfast bar. She paused long enough to make sandwiches for lunch, taking Devlin's out to him when he showed no sign of stopping for the meal. He accepted the plate from her with a quiet thank-you. Annalise didn't linger, sensing that he preferred to eat alone.

The afternoon was a continuance of the morning, with stacks of receipts soon covering the tiled bar. It was starting to register that Devlin had already spent a small fortune on the house. Everything had been paid for outright, whether it cost three dollars or three thousand.

Just where had he gotten this kind of money? she thought, fingering the bill for the fixtures in the master bath. She hadn't given it much thought until now, but he'd made no mention of going to work. His only work seemed to be on the house.

Maybe he just happened to be on vacation at the moment and was using the time to get some work done on his house? She frowned. Possible, but she didn't think so. Wouldn't he have made some mention of that when he asked her to work for him?

And come to think of it, how many people could afford to hire someone to sort receipts and deal with suppliers? She didn't doubt that he'd invented the job to help her get on her feet and she appreciated the generosity, nevertheless that sort of generosity didn't come cheap. The salary he had offered her wasn't extravagant, but it was more than a pittance.

It was none of her business, of course, where his money came from. Yet she couldn't help but be a bit curious. An inheritance, perhaps? Maybe his parents had been wealthy, like Bill's.

But Devlin didn't have any of the vaguely privileged air that had been so much a part of Bill. There'd been a sort of naiveté about her former husband that stemmed from his inability to believe that life didn't just naturally go the way he wanted it to. Bill had always been surprised and a little hurt when things went wrong.

There was nothing of that about Devlin. On the contrary, there was a certain wariness about him, as if he regarded life as more of an adversary, something he couldn't really afford to trust.

She put down the receipt, reminding herself again that Devlin's finances were not her concern. He'd asked her to organize his receipts, not handle his checkbook. But a little judicious probing couldn't do any harm.

"You really can cook." Devlin took another bite of fried chicken as if confirming the truth of his comment.

"You seemed to enjoy the pasta salad last night," Annalise reminded him. "Did you think that was all I could make?"

"Well, it could have been a fluke."

Perched on a ladder ten feet off the ground for most of the day, Devlin had had plenty of time to consider his understandable but unwanted reaction to Annalise. And he'd decided that the only way to handle it was to ignore it.

Part of the problem was simply that he wasn't accustomed to having an attractive woman constantly underfoot. Familiarity didn't only breed contempt. It also bred—well, familiarity. In a few days, he'd hardly notice Annalise as a woman.

It had all sounded quite simple when he was thinking about it this afternoon. Now, looking at the soft oval of her face, he felt a twinge of doubt. Maybe the air was thinner near the roofline and it had affected his brain.

It was hard to envision noticing Annalise St. John as anything other than a woman. There was something so feminine about her. It was there in the soft line of her jaw, in the delicate line of her neck.

He dragged his eyes away from her, frowning down at his plate. It was a simple matter of mind over libido.

"Do you have any family besides your sister?"

Annalise's question dragged Devlin's attention from his increasingly tangled thoughts. She was looking at him expectantly.

"Besides Kelly?" It took him a moment to shift gears. "No. Our mother died when Kelly was twelve."

"That's a tough age to lose a mother. How old were you?"

"Twenty-two. I'd already left home." *And had just started serving time for murder.* But there was no need to tell her that.

"What about your father? Did your sister stay with him?"

"What is this? Twenty questions?" Devlin pushed his plate away, contained violence in the gesture. He didn't like being reminded that Kelly had been left alone with that crazy old man. He didn't like remembering how badly he'd failed her when she'd needed him.

"I'm sorry." Annalise set her fork down, her appetite vanishing at his quick flare of anger. "I didn't mean to be nosy."

"No, wait." Devlin's hand closed over her wrist when she started to rise. "I'm the one who's sorry. I shouldn't have snarled at you like that."

"I didn't mean to pry." The smile she gave him held an edge of uncertainty that made Devlin's anger turn inward.

"You asked a perfectly normal question. You just . . . touched a nerve. That's all."

"I'm sorry."

She didn't say anything else, didn't give him an anticipatory look, didn't do anything to imply that she expected more of an explanation than he'd given. So why was it that he found himself talking again?

"Kelly was left with our . . . father." It was hard to say the word, hard to connect it with the harsh old man he remembered.

As far back as he could recall, it had been impossible to think of Seth Russell as his father. Fathers played softball with their sons and taught them how to drive. They didn't beat six-year-olds nearly unconscious, purging them of their sins.

"He was abusive," he said.

"How awful. Did he abuse you?"

"Yes." The simple word held a wealth of old memories, old hurts. "But he never hit Kelly. I stayed as long as I did because of Kelly, and he never hit her in all those years."

"How old were you when you left?"

"Eighteen." Devlin was hardly aware of Annalise's hand closing over his, her slender fingers trying to soothe the pain she sensed in him. "Kelly was eight. I didn't think she knew what had been happening, but she didn't cry when I told her I was leaving. She didn't ask me to stay."

"You were close?"

"Very. Mother was...well, she wasn't really around, even though she was physically there. I practically raised Kelly. I shouldn't have left. But I was afraid that if I stayed, I was going to kill him."

"I'm sure Kelly understood."

"Yeah. But that didn't do her a lot of good."

"Did he abuse her? After you left?"

"After Mother died." Devlin stood up, his rage too deep to allow him to stay still. He paced over to the back door, staring out the screen at the darkness beyond the porch light. "She doesn't talk about it much."

Annalise watched him, her eyes dark with compassion. She knew what it was to blame yourself when someone you loved was hurt. That deep-down feeling that you could have prevented it somehow. If only you'd said or done the right thing. If only...

And all the "if onlys" in the world couldn't change what had happened. She'd felt that way when her parents died, sure that if she'd just eaten her broccoli like her mother had asked her to do that last night, then their car wouldn't have skidded on a patch of ice and slammed into a telephone pole.

"You can't blame yourself," she said finally, wishing she had the right to go over and smooth the tension from his shoulders, to put her arms around him and help ease his pain.

"I can't?" He turned to look at her, his eyes dark and bitter. "I left her there. She was my little sister. She trusted me. I should have been there for her."

"Did you know what was happening?"

"No."

No, Kelly had written him cheerful little letters that never hinted at the hell she was living. She'd continued to write even when he'd stopped replying. He couldn't bear to tell her he was in prison, and he'd convinced himself that she would be better off thinking he'd forgotten her. But he hadn't been able to bring himself to cancel the post office box to which Kelly was writing. Nor to tell Reed to stop forwarding her letters. Sooner or later, she'd quit writing, leaving him completely alone.

She hadn't quit writing and he'd treasured each letter, reading them over and over again until they'd threatened to fall apart in his hands. He'd tried to imagine what she looked like as she grew from the freckled eight-year-old he'd left behind into a young woman. He'd pictured her going to dances, laughing with her friends, graduating high school.

Instead, she'd quit school rather than deal with their father's anger at her wasting her time getting an education. She'd endured his religious fanaticism, his periodic attempts to cleanse her of the devil that dwelled within every female by beating the sins from her.

She'd survived and managed to escape. She had a husband who worshiped the ground she walked on and a beautiful baby. When Clay started school, she planned to go to college.

"Where is Kelly now?' Annalise's question shook him out of his thoughts.

"She lives in Remembrance."

"Is she happy?"

"Yes." He could answer that without hesitation. "She's married and very happy."

"But you still blame yourself for what your father did."

"I should have been there," he said flatly, allowing no room for self-forgiveness.

"I seem to recall someone telling me recently that it didn't do much good to spend too much time worrying over the past," Annalise said thoughtfully. "Something about the past being past and nothing could change it."

Devlin stared at her, caught off guard by having his own words so neatly turned against him.

"Very clever," he said softly, his mouth starting to curve.

"I thought so." She looked so smug that his smile widened to something that might almost have been called a grin.

Annalise felt her breath catch. She'd wondered how he would look if he really smiled. She hadn't been prepared for the change the expression wrought in his lean features. If she'd thought him attractive before, she now realized the word was too anemic to apply. He was . . . devastating.

His smile revealed two deep dimples that creased his cheeks and banished the rather stern forbidding look he usually showed the world. He suddenly looked younger, approachable. The loneliness that haunted his eyes disappeared, replaced by a gleam that made them more blue than gray.

He looked altogether different, entirely too attractive. She felt a warming in the pit of her stomach that could have been, but wasn't, something perilously close to desire. She'd never felt anything quite like it before.

She swallowed hard and reminded herself that she had a life to get in order. And she certainly wasn't going to complicate the process by letting a mere sexual attraction get in the way.

"Okay, so now that you've heard my life story, what's yours?" Devlin leaned one hip against the counter and looked at her expectantly.

"Mine?" Annalise shrugged. "There isn't that much to tell." *At least not that much she was willing to tell.*

"Your parents?"

"Dead. They were killed in a car wreck when I was eight."

"That's tough."

"Yes. They didn't have any relatives who were willing to take me so I was put in a foster home." She ran her thumbnail along the edge of the table, remembering. "The Stomans. They were good people. I was with them for a year and then I went to live with the

Polachecks. They had eight children of their own. Sometimes, it seemed as if they had so many kids in and out of that house that they hardly knew which were theirs, and which were friends. I'd never been part of a big family. It was nice."

"How long were you with them?" Devlin asked, trying to picture her as a child. Thin, long legged, her face dominated by those big blue-green eyes. She must have had long hair even then, but it would have been finer, more flyaway.

"I stayed with the Polachecks almost two years. I think they'd have kept me longer, but Mr. Polacheck's company transferred him to a new job in another state. So then I went to stay with the Johnsons. They were considering adoption. I heard them talking about it, but they decided they wanted to adopt a younger child, instead of one that was already half-grown.

"Then it was the Mannings. That was for three years. They had a horse. Then the Sanfords, but that was only for a few months. It turned out Mr. Sanford had been borrowing money from his company's retirement fund.

"I stayed in a county facility for a while until they could find another family who was willing to take me. I was pretty old by then, and it's not easy to find anyone willing to take on an older child."

"You must have been ancient," Devlin agreed. "All of what, fourteen? Fifteen?"

She heard the anger he felt on behalf of the child she'd been and smiled. "It wasn't as bad as it sounds in the telling. All the families were nice to me. They did their best to make me feel at home."

"It couldn't have been easy to pull up roots every year or two, especially for a child."

"I got used to it. After a while, you learn not to let your roots grow too deep."

Devlin made a sound in his throat that sounded suspiciously like a growl. Annalise grinned. "Don't picture me as a pathetic orphan like something out of an old melodramatic silent movie. I was always fed and clothed. No one treated me badly."

The look he gave her suggested that their definition of being treated badly might differ, but he didn't argue with her.

"So did they find another family willing to take on such an *old* child?"

"Yes. The Millers. They had two small children of their own. They used to let me baby-sit." Her smile took on a wistful edge. "They were great kids. Sara Ann was just a baby and I used to rock her for hours."

The image of Annalise with an infant in her arms was surprisingly vivid. He shook his head to dispel it.

"How long did you stay with them?"

"A year and a half. I would have stayed longer, but Mrs. Miller found out she was pregnant again and they just didn't have room for me anymore.

"I went to stay with the McCleans after that. They were an older couple and the money they got for taking in foster children helped supplement their retirement income. I stayed with them until I graduated from high school."

Devlin waited for her to tell him what she'd done after high school, but she didn't seem to have anything more to say. She was tracing aimless patterns on the table with her forefinger, her eyes on the movement.

Of course he wasn't going to ask her to continue. No one respected another person's right to privacy more than he did. On the other hand, he had to admit to being curious.

"What happened after high school?" he asked finally.

She hesitated for so long he thought she was going to ignore the question.

"I got married." She lifted her shoulders in a quick shrug, as if to indicate how dull this piece of information was.

"Married?" There was no reason he should find it so startling, he reminded himself. He knew people who'd been married and divorced more than once by the time they reached their mid-twenties.

"I was nineteen. Too young, I suppose."

"Divorced?"

"Yes. Two years ago."

Devlin hadn't realized how anxious he was to hear her answer until she gave it. The idea that she might still be married was less than appealing. Only because he wouldn't like to think of her still tied to a relationship that had obviously ended, of course. It didn't bother him from a personal angle.

No, there was nothing personal in his relief. Nothing at all.

Chapter 7

The difficulty in keeping his distance from Annalise wasn't simply because she was living in his house, Devlin discovered. What made it so hard was that he liked her. He enjoyed her company. She understood the value of silence and didn't try to fill every minute with conversation.

And the more time he spent with her, the more he wanted to spend. He told himself it was the novelty of it. It wouldn't be long before he tired of having someone sharing his home. He should start looking for alternatives. He needed to find somewhere else for her to stay, another job.

With every day that passed, it was harder to see the pale wraith he'd pulled out of the river. She'd put on weight, enough to fill the hollows in her cheeks and add to the slender curves that made it difficult for him to go to sleep at night. Her hair held rich highlights now, catching the sun and seeming to hold its warmth in the heavy length of it.

Sometimes it took a conscious effort of will to keep from sliding his fingers into her hair to see if it felt as warm and soft as it looked. No matter how hard he tamped down the sexual awareness he felt, he had only to look at her to feel it surging through him.

He was losing sleep, and there were times when he thought he might be losing his sanity. Obviously he had to get her settled somewhere else, a place where he didn't see her first thing in the morning, when the sleepy look of her eyes made him want to kiss her. Where he couldn't hear her run a bath every night and then torture himself with imagining her in that bath.

Ben Masters would be the person to call. He'd called him the day after Annalise's arrival and told him that she'd be staying with him for a few days. Ben had emphasized that Devlin was to call if there was anything he could do to help.

The cynical side of him suggested that the doctor's eagerness to help might have been aided by the size of the donation he'd made. But he didn't really believe that. Kelly had told him enough about Ben to make him willing to believe that the other man really cared. A man didn't spend as much time working with patients who couldn't pay as Ben did unless he was truly dedicated or running for political office.

He hadn't called Ben back, but he was sure the doctor would help him find a position for Annalise if he asked him to. That was the logical thing to do. He liked her and he'd miss her company, at least for a day or two. But the fact was, having her around was not conducive to the sort of peaceful life he'd spent almost a year establishing.

Still he didn't call Ben. And he didn't mention anything to Annalise about the possibility of finding her another place to stay. He told himself that he didn't want to upset her. She had come so far in such a short time. He didn't want to do anything that might bring that haunting emptiness to her eyes.

So he didn't do anything about getting her out of his life.

Though Devlin had driven into town three or four times to pick up things he needed for the house, Annalise didn't make the trip until after she'd been staying with him for nearly two weeks. Her car had been running for most of that time, but she hadn't felt any urge to leave the house that had become almost a sanctuary.

"I was thinking that some flowers along the drive right in front of the house would look nice," she said, glancing at Devlin uncertainly. She didn't want him to think she was pushing her way in where she didn't belong.

Devlin finished pulling the truck into a parking space before looking at her. He nodded. "That sounds nice. What have you got in mind?"

"I don't now for sure. I thought maybe, if you didn't mind, we could stop at a nursery. I noticed one on the way into town. We could take a look at what they've got."

"Sounds good." He glanced at his watch. "Will two hours give you enough time to get whatever you need?"

"I can buy a pair of jeans in less than two hours."

"Well, maybe you'll think of something else you need. There's a bookstore half a block down on the right. I've got an order to pick up there. Why don't we meet there in two hours?"

"Okay." Annalise climbed out of the truck, slamming the heavy door shut before moving around to the front of the vehicle. Devlin paused on the sidewalk, glancing at the list he'd just pulled out of his shirt pocket.

Standing there, wearing jeans and a soft gray cotton shirt with the sleeves rolled up over his forearms, he looked wonderfully solid. Annalise caught the inside of her lower lip between her teeth, holding back the urge to suggest that she could tag along with him. She could carry buckets of paint or bags of cement—whatever he liked. Just as long as he didn't leave her alone.

But that was ridiculous. He wasn't abandoning her in the middle of New York City. Remembrance, Indiana, was a peaceful, not very large town where the greatest danger likely to befall her was getting a ticket for jaywalking.

"You'll be all right?" As if he could read the doubts chasing one another around her mind, Devlin looked up from his list to pin her with eyes that saw more than they should.

"Sure," she said, forcing a bright smile. "It looks like a great little town."

"It's pretty peaceful." Devlin glanced at the shops that lined the street. "You should be able to find just about anything you need. There's a clothing store right across the street."

"Don't worry about me. I'll be fine."

When he hesitated, she gave him another smile, hoping he couldn't read the stark terror she was feeling. She hadn't realized how much her sense of security had come to depend on his presence until she found herself about to be left alone in the middle of a strange town.

"You have enough money?" he asked abruptly.

"Yes. I already told you that the salary you're paying is too generous for what I'm doing. I have *plenty* of money."

"Good." He glanced at his watch again but made no move to leave. "Are you sure you'll be all right?"

It hit her suddenly that he had as many doubts about leaving her on her own as she did about being on her own. The knowledge stiffened her spine. Since when had she become so helpless that she couldn't buy a pair of jeans without a keeper?

Her fingers tightened on the strap of the cheap plastic purse, and her chin tilted up a fraction of an inch. Her smile lost some of its forced edge.

"I'll be fine," she told him again. "I'll meet you at the bookstore in two hours."

Lifting one hand in a casual wave, she turned and walked briskly off down the sidewalk. Devlin stayed where he was, watching her. She didn't look back, not even when she paused to check traffic before stepping into the crosswalk.

She looked very small and vulnerable. Maybe it was the way she was dressed. She was wearing a pair of jeans whose worn look had come from wear and not a designer's factory and one of his T-shirts, which was so large it made her look as if she were playing dress-up. Kelly's sneakers completed the outfit.

He forced himself to turn away, long strides carrying him in the opposite direction. Annalise was a grown woman. She didn't need him to play bodyguard. She'd pulled herself together to an amazing degree these past couple of weeks. He was sure a couple of hours alone wasn't going to do her any harm.

If only he could get it out of his head that she'd looked absolutely terrified just before she walked away.

"Actually, I really enjoyed myself." Annalise gave him a shy smile. "I don't know if you could tell, but I was scared to death there for a minute."

"It didn't show," Devlin told her without a second's hesitation. He didn't have to take his eyes off the road to see her smile. He could feel it.

"Good." She rubbed her fingers absently over the surface of her new purse, a scarlet canvas clutch. "I felt really stupid. It isn't as if I've never been shopping alone before. I guess it's just that these last two weeks, I've started putting myself back together again. I wasn't sure I was ready to go out into the real world, even for something as basic as shopping. But it felt really good."

"Did you get everything you needed?" He cast a doubtful look at the two sacks at her feet.

"I didn't need much." She was quiet for a moment, staring out at the fields that lined the road. "You know, I'll never be able to repay you for all you've done for me, Devlin. I don't now what I'd have done if you hadn't—"

"One more word and you walk the rest of the way," he interrupted.

"Okay." She slid him a quick glance and dared to add one more sentence. "I just want to thank you," she said hurriedly.

"You've already thanked me." Her gratitude made him uncomfortable. He didn't want Annalise feeling grateful to him. He wanted her... hell, face it, jerk, you just plain want her.

His hands tightened on the wheel, the knuckles showing white for a moment before he forced his fingers to relax. Over the past two weeks, he'd gotten more experience than he'd ever hoped to have in quelling lustful thoughts.

There was little conversation during the remainder of the drive home. Annalise was content to savor the feeling that she'd faced a challenge and triumphed. Devlin was wondering how many cold showers a man could take before doing permanent physical damage. Something had to give soon. He only hoped it wouldn't be his sanity.

He parked the truck next to the house. He had to unload the truck bed, but he decided to change his shoes first. When the frame was first going up, he'd once dropped an armload of two-by-fours on his foot. The results had convinced him that the best way to move quantities of lumber was in a pair of sturdy boots.

Annalise preceded him into the house, going straight to the guest room to put away her purchases. She was snipping the tags from a crisp new pair of jeans when she heard Devlin call her name.

"Annalise? I think you should come look at this." There was a curious note in his voice, not exactly urgency but something more than a casual summons.

Annalise dropped the jeans onto the bed and left her room. Devlin was still talking, but he wasn't using any tone she'd ever heard from him. He was speaking too softly for her to make out words, but there was a low, soothing quality to his voice that was like stroking her hand over a warm blanket.

She followed the sound into his bedroom and saw him kneeling in front of the closet. She knew what was in the closet and who he was talking to even before she sank to her knees beside him.

Beauty lay on her side, smack in the center of the closet floor. She was lying on a dress shirt that had probably slipped off the hanger. It was a sure bet it was never going to be the same, but no one seemed to mind. Nestled against Beauty's stomach were four kittens, three grey like their mother and one a startling snowy white. All four were busily nursing with a concentration contrary to their size and helplessness.

Annalise felt tears come to her eyes, and her mouth curved upward in a foolish smile.

"Look," she said in a hushed voice, as if Devlin might not have seen his closet's new occupants. "She had her litter."

"It's about time. If she'd gotten any bigger, she would have popped like a balloon." Devlin's gruff words were at odds with the gentle finger he ran over Beauty's head. "What a good girl you are," he told the new mother. "Look at your beautiful babies."

Beauty regarded them with a look that could only be described as smug. She knew her kittens were beautiful, but she was pleased that these big, clumsy creatures were capable of seeing the obvious.

"They're so perfect," Annalise whispered, reaching out to stroke her fingertip over one tiny back. The kitten ignored her, intent on finishing her meal.

"Of course they're perfect. Look what a perfect mom they've got." Beauty allowed Devlin to rub behind her ear, accepting his praise as her due.

If Annalise had had her doubts about whether or not Devlin minded that he'd acquired a houseguest and a pet in the same twenty-four-hour period, she was reassured now. He'd fed Beauty and never offered any objection to her presence, either by word or look, but he'd also never paid much attention to the cat. She'd thought that perhaps he was one of those people who were not entirely at ease with animals.

But he was perfectly comfortable with Beauty now, talking to her in that soft voice, making it clear that her efforts were not unappreciated.

Looking at the tiny kittens, Annalise felt fresh tears sting her eyes. Four new lives. It wouldn't be long before they'd be venturing out of their home in the closet and getting underfoot, making complete nuisances of themselves.

Life was a constant cycle of renewal. No matter what happened, there was always a new cycle beginning somewhere. It was a thought at once humbling and reassuring.

His attention drawn by her silence, Devlin turned his head to look at her. Their eyes met, his more open than usual with the simple pleasure he took in the new family, hers more green than blue with emotion.

He stared at her, caught by the hidden depths in her eyes. What was it about her eyes that always hinted at mysteries he'd never quite understand?

A strand of hair had fallen loose from the clip with which she'd drawn the heavy length back and lay against her cheek. He reached up to put it in place. Only somehow, his fingers were loosening the clasp. It hit the floor with a sharp click. It could have exploded like dynamite and neither of them would have noticed.

Annalise's hair spilled over his fingers like living silk. Without taking his eyes from hers, he drew a handful of it forward so that it fell across her breast, a pale contrast to the navy T-shirt she wore.

Her eyes widened and he could hear an odd little catch to her breathing, but she didn't move back, didn't utter a word of protest as his hand closed over the sensitive nape of her neck.

His eyes locked on hers, Devlin drew her forward. Only in the last heartbeat before their lips met did her gaze flicker, her lashes coming down to shield her eyes from his.

But then his mouth was on hers, and he didn't have to read her reaction in her eyes. He could taste it in the way her lips softened beneath his, hear it in the barely audible sigh that escaped her.

Devlin had been fantasizing for almost two weeks about what kissing her would be like. But no fantasy could begin to compare with the reality. And the reality was that she was a taste of heaven on earth. And no fantasy could have prepared him for the explosion a simple kiss touched off between them.

His mouth firmed, his head tilting to deepen the kiss. Her lips opened to him, an invitation he didn't try to resist. Her tongue came up to meet his, her response as quick and hard as his own.

Still on his knees, he drew her closer, wanting to feel her with every pore of his being. Annalise's hands settled on his shoulders, hesitating uncertainly for a moment before her fingers crept into the thick darkness of his hair. She molded her fingers to the back of his skull, the simple touch fanning the flames of his need even higher.

Devlin left one hand buried in the irresistible silk of her hair. The other traveled down her back, tracing her spine through the thin knit of the T-shirt before coming to rest on her backside.

She complied easily when he pressed her closer, shifting his knees apart so that the cradle of her femininity pressed against the rock-hard proof of his desire.

His mouth caught the small gasp that escaped her as she felt the strength of his need. Devlin's mouth was avid on hers. All the hunger he'd been suppressing was battering at the doors of his control.

He wanted to press her back onto the floor and strip away the frustrating layers of clothing between them. He wanted to feel her thighs cradling him, feel her body accepting him in the most intimate of embraces.

He wanted to hear her cry out his name in her pleasure, to see her writhing beneath him, her body burning with the same need he felt.

The very strength of that need—the realization that he was within a millisecond of losing control—brought Devlin to his senses. He felt as if he were teetering on the brink of a huge chasm. On the other side lay as near to paradise as it was possible to find in the mortal world. But to get there, he had to risk giving up the control that had kept him sane through all the dark hours in his life.

That rigid refusal to give even a fraction of himself over into someone else's power had enabled him to survive his childhood and eight years in prison. And he couldn't possibly make love to Annalise and retain that control. He wanted her too badly.

Hammering down the screaming need in his gut, Devlin ended the kiss. His hands moved to grip her shoulders, drawing her away even though it felt as if he were pulling off a layer of his own skin.

Their eyes met, hers reflecting a startled wonder that made him ache to pull her back into his arms. But he wasn't going to do that.

For a moment, Annalise saw her own wonder reflected in Devlin's eyes and knew that the kiss had been as much of a revelation to him as it had been to her. Then the shutters came down, shutting her out, closing him inside.

"Annalise, I—"

She interrupted quickly. "Well, that was certainly a surprise." She scrambled to her feet as she spoke, quickly putting a little distance between them.

"A surprise," Devlin repeated. He stood more slowly, his feet slightly apart as if he were bracing for a fight. She forced herself to ignore the solid bulge at his fly that made it clear that he might have shut her out but his body hadn't quite gotten the message yet.

"Of course, it was only to be expected," she said brightly. She bent down to pick up her hair clip and swept her hair back into it with quick, nervous movements, hoping he couldn't see that her fingers were trembling.

"It was?"

"Of course. I'd been expecting it. Hadn't you? I mean, here we are, living here together. And you know what they say about proximity."

She edged toward the door, aware that she was babbling like an idiot. But she had to stop him from speaking. She couldn't bear to hear what he'd say, though she couldn't have said exactly what that might be.

"Proximity." He didn't seem capable of anything beyond repeating her words.

"Of course. Well, I'm glad that's out of the way. Now we can get on with things without wondering what it would be like to kiss one another. Thanks for calling me in to see the kittens."

She could feel her inane smile starting to crack around the edges. "I should finish putting away the things I bought today," she said, as if she'd brought back cartons of things instead of only two medium-sized sacks.

She darted out of the door before Devlin could say anything, though from the stunned look on his face she doubted he could have found any words.

Annalise reached the sanctuary of her bedroom, closing the door behind her and leaning up against it. The tight smile disappeared. She bit her lower lip when it threatened to tremble.

For all the nonsense she'd babbled to Devlin, no one could have been less prepared for what had just happened than she had been. Oh, she'd been aware of an occasional twinge of interest. You couldn't live with a man as attractive as Devlin Russell and not notice him.

She'd even had an occasional dreamy thought about what it might be like if he kissed her. But her vague imaginings of him gently pressing his lips to hers hadn't prepared her for the reality.

What had happened to her in there? She'd never felt that kind of blazing need in her life. Certainly never with Bill. She'd never even imagined she was capable of such feelings.

Bill had been her only lover, and she'd found sex with him a warm, friendly thing. Pleasant enough that she'd never had a reason to object to his advances, even if it hardly made the stars fall from the sky.

If she'd had her moments of wondering if there shouldn't be a little more to it than the vague pleasure of knowing that he'd found his satisfaction, she'd pushed the thoughts away, afraid to find any faults with her marriage. She'd lost too many people in her life to risk losing her husband by complaining about their sex life. She wasn't really the passionate sort anyway. Any lack she felt was undoubtedly in her.

But she couldn't believe that anymore. Moments ago, she'd discovered that she was very much the passionate sort. In Devlin's arms, in his kiss, a whole new side of her had been revealed. She hadn't just responded to his hunger. She'd felt a hunger all her own.

She pressed her fingers to her lips. If he'd wanted to take her right there on the floor, she'd have welcomed him. Even now, her body was still tingling with a new awareness.

"Forget it," she whispered fiercely. "You saw the look in his eyes. He doesn't want this any more than you do. You don't want it." The words were more order than statement.

Proximity. She'd been babbling when she'd told Devlin that was all it was, but the more she thought about it, the more sense it made. As she'd said, they were living here together, seeing each other constantly. It was only natural that a certain sexual tension would develop.

But that's all it was, and if they just ignored it, it would go away.

But if ignoring it was the cure, it was going to take longer than she'd hoped. Devlin wasn't the sort of man who was easy to ignore under any circumstances, but the kiss they'd shared made it almost impossible.

And as if to add to the problem, summer swept over Indiana, elbowing spring aside practically overnigh⁺ The temperatures rose accordingly. More often than not, Devlin's shirt disappeared sometime before noon, leaving Annalise with a fine, unwanted view of his muscled torso.

But the worst thing was not the sight of Devlin's truly splendid physique. The worst thing was the new tension that had sprung up between them. By tacit agreement, neither made any reference to the momentary madness they'd shared the day Beauty's kittens entered the world. But it was there in every glance that passed between them.

Beneath the most innocuous of conversations ran a fine tension, an awareness that didn't disappear with being ignored. The meals they shared were no longer relaxed interludes where the conversation might center on an idea Devlin had had for the house or a book one of them had read.

Conversation grew stilted, punctuated by long silences that neither wanted to break. It was the loss of Devlin's friendship that bothered her more than anything else. She hadn't realized how much she'd enjoyed the rather reserved companionship he offered until it was gone.

The sad thing was, she didn't know how to go about regaining it. They couldn't go back and erase the kiss. It had happened. There was no changing that.

Sleeping together wasn't the answer, either. Though she was willing to admit, somewhat painfully, that if Devlin suggested it, she probably wouldn't hesitate very long.

But he wouldn't suggest it. Not unless he found a way to let her inside the wall he kept around himself, or at least partway in. She'd seen the look in his eyes when he ended the kiss. Dazed as she'd been, she recognized when someone was shutting her out.

It had hurt, but she knew it wasn't really personal with Devlin. She believed the wall was a deeply rooted part of him, a protection he let very few people inside. She knew what it was to put up walls. And she knew how badly it could hurt to let someone inside.

She was rather gloomily contemplating this thought a few days after The Kiss—she'd come to think of it in capitals. There was a storm building up; huge black thunderheads had been gathering all afternoon, making the air thick and muggy with the promise of rain.

It was the sort of weather that made your skin feel too tight, as if the electricity in the air had somehow gotten beneath it, drawing it closer about your bones.

Devlin was working outside. Annalise was supposedly entering figures into the accounting book he'd bought for that purpose when they visited Remembrance. Actually she'd spent a great deal more time staring at nothing than she had writing anything.

When she heard the sound of a car coming down the driveway, curiosity at least momentarily dislodged the frustrated circle of her thinking. She got up from the table and went to the front door.

A bright red compact had just pulled to a stop in front of the house, and a slender brunette was getting out. Annalise started to open the door, half thinking that the woman might be lost and hoping to get directions. Before she could push the screen open, the stranger's face broke into a grin.

"Dev!"

Devlin came into sight, shrugging into his shirt as he strode toward the woman. But it wasn't the sight of his bare chest that made Annalise's breath catch. It was the warmth of his smile—a genuine smile that lit up his entire face.

"Midget! What are you doing all the way out here?" Before Annalise had a chance to regain her breath, it was stolen from her again by seeing the taciturn, unapproachable Devlin Russell pick the brunette up and swing her around.

"Stop it, you fiend! You're all dirty." The reprimand might have been more effective if she hadn't been laughing up at him.

Midget? It didn't sound like the sort of pet name you'd give a lover. More like the kind of thing you might call a little sister. Was this Kelly?

She lingered in the doorway, watching shamelessly as Devlin lowered the other woman to the ground but kept his arm around her shoulders.

"I was visiting a site that Dan's working on, and on the way home, I realized that your place wasn't that far out of my way, so I thought I'd drop by. You don't mind, do you, Dev?"

"Of course not. You know you're always welcome."

"I've extended the same invitation to you," she said, a hint of tartness in the tone. "I haven't noticed you taking me up on it."

Devlin shrugged. "I've been busy. You know how it is, Kelly."

"I know exactly how it is. You're unsociable, Devlin Russell. Do you know how long it's been since you've been to see us? Clay is going to forget who you are."

"No, he won't. He's too smart. Is he with you?" Devlin dropped his arm from her shoulder, bending to look in the car window.

Clay? Who was Clay? The way the sun slanted across the windshield made it impossible for Annalise to see inside. It didn't prevent her from seeing the wriggling infant that Kelly lifted out of a car seat a moment later.

"Remember your Uncle Devlin, sweetie pie?"

"Of course he does. How's my favorite nephew?" Devlin held out his hands to take the baby from her, but Kelly held back.

"He needs to be changed," she warned.

"That's okay. We can change him in the house." He took the baby from her, holding him with none of the awkward self-consciousness that most men felt with an infant.

Annalise hardly noticed. When Kelly lifted the child from the car, the breath left her lungs with painful speed. She drew back from the door, feeling her skin flush and then pale.

She'd thought she was over the worst of it. She'd been so sure she'd moved beyond the agony that flooded her now. Oh, God, they were coming inside. Without giving it a second's thought, she darted across the living room and into her bedroom, shutting the door and leaning against it.

She heard Devlin and Kelly enter the house. She prayed that Devlin wouldn't feel it necessary to come and find her. She'd been curious about his sister and had thought it would be interesting to meet her. But that was before she knew Kelly had a baby. She couldn't meet her now. She couldn't go out there and smile and make polite conversation, trying not to look at Kelly's son.

Please, let Devlin just forget all about her.

"Whose car is that next to the house?" Kelly's curious voice carried easily through the door. Annalise held her breath, waiting for Devlin's reply. Let him say he'd bought it as a second car, that it had fallen out of the sky.

Devlin's answer seemed slow in coming, but it wasn't the one she'd been praying for. "It belongs to a... friend of mine. She's been staying with me for a couple of weeks."

"She?"

"Don't get any bright ideas, Midget. She's a friend."

Annalise pressed herself closer against the door as she heard Devlin's footsteps crossing the living room.

"Annalise?" He tapped lightly on the door. Obviously he thought she might be taking a nap. He couldn't possibly know that she was cowering here like someone about to be dragged before a firing squad. "Annalise?"

She could just pretend she was asleep. He'd go away then. Or he might open the door to check on her. And then she'd have to explain why she'd been pretending she didn't hear him.

"Yes?" The one word was almost impossible to force out.

"Kelly's here. My sister," he added, in case she'd forgotten.

"I'll...be right out," she managed.

Devlin lingered on the other side of the door, as if he'd heard something in her voice that didn't seem quite right.

She released her breath on a sigh that was only a hair's breadth away from being a sob. Straightening away from the door, she smoothed her hands over the soft pink T-shirt she wore over her jeans. She pinched her cheeks, knowing they must be too pale.

She could do this. All she had to do was go to out there and make a few minutes of polite conversation and then make some excuse to leave. Not for a moment, not even for a split second, would she look at Kelly's baby. Not everyone oohed and aahed over infants.

Her knees were trembling as she pulled open the bedroom door and stepped out into the living room. The first thing she saw was the baby, freshly diapered and overall clad, crawling across the floor in her direction.

It took every ounce of willpower she had to keep from darting back into the bedroom and shutting the door. She dragged her eyes from his small figure and forced a smile that she hoped didn't look as sickly as it felt.

Afterward she could remember very little of her meeting with Kelly Remington. She must have responded in all the right places and said the right things, because no one seemed to notice anything wrong.

When Kelly picked up Clay, Annalise felt an actual, physical ache. Her arms hurt. She couldn't keep her eyes from the infant, who seemed reasonably content to view the world from the safety of his mother's arms.

"Would you like to hold him?"

At Kelly's words, Annalise's eyes snapped up to meet hers, wondering if she'd somehow revealed the painful hunger the baby made her feel. But Kelly only gave her a friendly smile and held Clay out. Vaguely Annalise was aware of the questioning look Devlin sent her, as if he sensed something of the turmoil she was feeling.

She wasn't going to take the baby, of course. Holding him would only make the pain worse, add to the emptiness that gnawed at her. She'd smile and thank Kelly and shake her head. She really wasn't the baby type, she'd say.

She saw her hands go out as if they belonged to someone else. Clay's body felt strong and sturdy in her hands. He studied her with bright blue eyes and then gave her a wide grin, confident that the sight of his two brand-new front teeth would make her a slave for life, just as it had done with everyone else in his life.

Annalise felt her breath catch, remembering another baby, another toothy grin. She drew him closer. He smelled of baby powder and formula. He felt like heaven. If she closed her eyes, he could be another baby, a little less sturdy, her eyes a softer blue.

"He's...he's very sweet," she said, aware that the silence had stretched on too long and both Devlin and Kelly were looking at her.

"We like him," Kelly said lightly.

"He's so strong. So healthy." Annalise tugged his overalls into better order, aware that her fingers were visibly trembling. "So healthy," she said again.

"Yes, he is." Kelly glanced at her brother, her dark eyes questioning, but Devlin could only shrug. That something was very wrong was obvious, but he didn't know what it was any more than she did.

After a moment, Annalise handed the baby back to his mother, her hands dropping immediately to her sides, her fingers curling into her palms.

"He's wonderful," she told Kelly, her bright smile at odds with the tears she didn't seem to realize were trickling down her cheeks.

"Thank you," Kelly said. "Are you all right?"

"Yes. Yes, of course." Annalise looked around as if she weren't quite sure where she was. "I...excuse me. I have to...excuse me."

She all but ran from the room, darting through the kitchen and out the back door, the screen slamming behind her. As if it were a cue, thunder rumbled, the sound closer now. A cool breeze skipped through the back door, stirring the papers on the kitchen table, sending them drifting to the floor.

Chapter 8

"What was that all about?"

Devlin dragged his gaze from the back door to his sister's bewildered face.

"I don't know," he said slowly. And it was none of his business, he reminded himself. He was trying to put distance between himself and Annalise, not get even more deeply involved. But her pain had been so vivid.

"You probably ought to get on the road before the rain really gets started." He reached out to give his nephew an absent nudge on the chin.

"And maybe you should see what's wrong with Annalise."

"Maybe." He was going to let her work this out without him, he reminded himself.

"And don't think I don't still have a million questions about her," Kelly added, gathering up Clay's diaper bag on the way to the door.

"Fine." Devlin's gaze drifted to the back door.

He saw his sister off, watching her car until it turned onto the main road. The rain started as he headed back into the house. He stood in the middle of the living room, reminding himself that he didn't want to get any more involved in Annalise St. John's problems.

She was far from suicidal now. Whatever had set her off, it wasn't his problem. She probably wouldn't even welcome his concern.

He went into the kitchen and began to pick up the receipts that had landed on the floor, setting them on the table and putting the account book on top of them. Outside, the rain was increasing in intensity.

Annalise hadn't been wearing anything remotely suited to a rainstorm. She'd be soaked to the skin in minutes. Staring out at the rain, he remembered the night he'd first seen her, standing on the riverbank, her shoulders slumped as if the weight of the world rested on them. She was still so vulnerable.

Cursing, he strode across the kitchen and slammed out the back door. He was just going to make sure she was all right, he told himself. She was sort of his responsibility, wasn't she? He'd make sure she was all right, and then he was going to take a nice hot shower and let her deal with her own problems.

It wasn't a hard rain, but it was a steady downpour that soaked everything it touched almost immediately. Devlin's light shirt was drenched before he was halfway across the backyard.

Annalise wasn't hard to find. The pink of her T-shirt stood out like a beacon through the falling rain. She was standing at the bottom of the long yard, staring down at the river.

Devlin felt fear cut off his breathing. His long stride lengthened into a sprint. What if he'd been wrong in thinking she wouldn't kill herself? What if she jumped into the river before he reached her?

He slowed as he neared her, feeling his heart start to beat again. She was well back from the bank. She had her arms crossed around her waist and her shoulders were hunched as if her pain were an actual physical burden. But she didn't look as though she'd been contemplating drowning her sorrows.

Adrenaline still surged in him as he stopped beside her. At first he thought she was so wrapped in sorrow that she wasn't even aware of his presence. But then she turned her head to look at him, her tears mingling with the rain.

"It hurts," she said quietly.

The simple, almost childlike statement sent a shaft of pain through Devlin's heart. Acting on instinct, he reached out, putting his arms around her and drawing her to him.

"I know." And he did know. Not what had caused her pain specifically, but he knew what it was to hurt so much the pain was almost unbearable.

Turning, Annalise leaned against him like a tired child, her cheek resting against his wet shirt, her hands settling on his hips.

"It hurts so much. Sometimes, I feel as if I'm dead inside, as if all that's left of me is the pain."

Her words sliced into him, making him feel her pain as his own. With both hands he cupped her cheeks, tilting her face up until her eyes met his.

"You're not dead, Annalise. And the pain gets easier to bear."

There was no lightening of the darkness in her eyes. "Make it go away, Devlin. Make it stop hurting." Her lower lip trembled and Devlin's heart broke into a thousand pieces.

Hardly conscious of what he was doing, wanting only to ease her hurt, even if it meant taking the hurt and making it his, he lowered his mouth to hers.

He intended the kiss as comfort. He intended it to show her that she wasn't alone. He wanted to make her see that she was alive, that she could feel more than the emptiness and disillusion.

But whatever his intentions had been, they were scattered to the winds by her response. Her arms came up to circle his neck, her body arching against his. He'd offered a way for her to forget the pain, if only temporarily, and she was grabbing at it with both hands.

Despite the kiss they'd already shared, Devlin was caught off balance by the way passion seemed to almost literally explode between them. In the space of a heartbeat, everything was forgotten but the feel of Annalise in his arms, the taste of her on his lips.

He caught her closer, his mouth slanting hungrily across hers. Her response was every bit as urgent. Her fingers curled into the damp thickness of his hair, dragging him closer still.

There was no time to think. No time to wonder if this was the right thing. No time to draw back. The only thing possible was to feel her with every fiber of his being.

The rain had soaked their clothes, plastering the fabric to their skin. Devlin's hands slid down to cup Annalise's hips, lifting her off her feet as he pulled her against his thighs. She whimpered low in her throat as she felt his need pressed against her. She arched into him, making him curse the fact that they were still dressed.

He started to ease her back down to her feet, intending to take her into the house. But she had no intention of letting him go, even for that long. Her legs parted and came up to circle his lean hips, even as her arms tightened around his neck.

Devlin groaned, his hands shifting automatically to support her. The only way they could have been more intimately entwined was if they'd been naked. He could feel the heart of her pressed against the aching bulge of him. In that instant, he'd have given a year of his life to have their clothing vanish, to be able to slide himself into her.

He started up to the house, Annalise wrapped around him like the most sensuous of blankets. By the time he pulled open the screen door, the blood was pounding in his temples. If the roof had collapsed at that moment, it wouldn't have made him slow his pace. He had to have her. Whether it was in his bed or standing in the middle of a rainstorm or on the floor, he had to have her or go mad.

He was no longer concerned with keeping his distance—it was too late for that. And he didn't care that he might be getting too involved. His involvement was already too deep. All that mattered at this moment was easing the burning ache in his loins.

He stopped next to his bed, easing Annalise to the floor. She would have protested, but he was already stripping her T-shirt over her head. When he fumbled with the front clasp of her bra, she disposed of it herself, tossing the garment into a corner.

Devlin's hands came up, cupping the sweet dampness of her breasts, feeling the nipples hard and taut against his palms. He wanted to taste them, wanting to lick the rain from them. But Annalise's hands were already unzipping her jeans, stripping them down off her hips and then reaching for his.

"Hurry," she whispered. When the buttons defeated her shaking fingers, she cupped her hand over him, drawing a guttural groan from him.

"Hurry," she said again.

Devlin's fingers worked the buttons of his jeans. He shoved them down, releasing the heavy length of his manhood. Annalise's fingers closed around him and he thought he'd surely explode.

"You're going to kill me," he said, only half-joking. His hands closed over her wrist, drawing her away.

He eased her back onto the bed, following her down. His hands stroked the length of her sides, savoring the silken feel of her skin. But Annalise twisted beneath him, opening her legs, her ankles coming up to press against his hips.

Devlin groaned and fought the urge to take her invitation. This wasn't how he wanted their first time to be. He wanted to slow the pace, savor every minute.

"We've got all the time in the world," he whispered.

She stared up at him, her eyes dark with need and some emotion he was too dazed to put a name to. She shook her head, scattering her damp hair across the covers.

"Now, Devlin. Please, now."

"Annalise . . . ah, sweetheart." She'd reached between them and closed her hand over the swollen length of him, drawing him forward until he rested against her dampness.

"Now," she whispered fiercely, her hips arching as if to force him to take her.

Devlin's control shattered into a million pieces. With a soft curse that was almost a prayer, he slid his burning length into her. She gasped as her body stretched to accommodate his.

She fit him as if made for him alone. Her softness surrounded him, changing what had been near pain to a painfully intense pleasure. Devlin pressed his forehead to the pillow beside her head, struggling for some shred of control.

Despite her eagerness, she hadn't been quite ready for him. He'd felt it in the sharp gasp, in the tightness of the flesh that sheathed him. He wanted to empty himself in her, to feel an easing of the ache that had gnawed at him for weeks. But he wanted her to feel that same pleasure. It was a journey much sweeter if they made it together.

But Annalise wasn't interested in him taking his time. She wanted only to rush headlong into the sweet oblivion she could feel just out of reach. Only that would take away her pain, ease the feeling that she'd never be wholly alive again. She arched her hips into his, drawing her legs up to circle his waist so that she took him even deeper.

"Don't." Devlin lifted himself on his arms, his fingers knotted over the blankets as he struggled for control. "Slow down, sweetheart."

"I don't want to slow down," she whispered, her hips arching again as her fingers trailed down the length of his spine. "Please, Devlin. Please."

She lifted her head to plant soft kisses across his chest. Her mouth found the flat nub of his nipple and her tongue came out to taste it. Devlin shuddered, feeling his fragile control dissolving like mist before a hot sun. Her teeth scored him lightly and he surrendered with a groan.

His hips rose and fell, feeling her flesh enfold him in the sweetest of embraces. Through the pounding in his temples, he knew that something wasn't right. She was rushing him along, her hands and legs holding him, dragging him headlong into the madness. But somewhere he'd lost her and it was too late to stop now.

He arched against her, grinding his teeth together against a pleasure so intense it must surely approach death. But the intensity of his release was clouded by the knowledge that he'd reached it alone.

He lowered his head to the pillow beside her, his breath shuddering in and out of him. He felt her legs drop to the bed, releasing him from their sweet prison. As his mind slowly cleared, he was aware that a deep anger was rolling in to fill the spaces temporarily emptied of need.

He was angry with Annalise for rushing their lovemaking, for refusing to let him take the time to make sure she was with him all the way. Most of all he was furious with himself for letting her do it.

Devlin rolled away from her, sensing the slight discomfort his withdrawal caused her. It only added to his anger.

They lay there without speaking, the room completely silent but for the steady patter of the rain. It was left to Annalise to break the silence. With an inaudible excuse, she started to get off the bed.

Devlin's hand caught her before she'd managed to sit up, pushing her implacably back against the pillow. He loomed over her, his shoulders blocking out her view of the room, leaving her with nothing to look at but his angry gray eyes.

"You want to tell me what the hell that was all about?" he demanded fiercely.

Annalise closed her eyes, but she couldn't shut out the knowledge that he had a right to be upset. She'd used him to try to blot out the pain.

"I'm sorry," she whispered.

"Sorry?" Illogically his anger immediately darted away from her, centering solely on what he saw as his own monumental failure. "You're sorry because I acted like a randy sixteen-year-old?'' He released her, rolling away to sit on the edge of the bed, his shoulders taut.

"I pushed you," she said, sitting up. She tugged the sheet up over her breasts. "I had no right to use you like that."

"Use me?" Devlin turned to face her, drawing one knee up on the bed. "*You* used *me?*"

"Yes." She lowered her eyes.

Devlin sighed, feeling all his anger drain away. "You didn't use me, Annalise. I've been aching to make love to you practically from the moment I saw you. But this isn't exactly how I'd have liked it to go."

"It's all right." She reached out to touch his arm, withdrawing her fingers quickly.

"No, it isn't. I wanted you with me."

"With you? I was with you." She blinked at him, confused.

Devlin stared at her. She didn't even realize what she'd lost in her headlong rush.

"What do you mean?" she asked.

"Never mind." It wasn't something he could possibly sit here and explain to her. Maybe, with luck, he'd get a second chance to show her what he meant. Because there was no sense in pretending that he didn't want to make love to her again. And again.

"What happened, Annalise? Why were you so upset? What was it about seeing Kelly and the baby that hurt you so much?"

Her eyes dropped from his to stare at the rumpled covers between them. She owed him an explanation. No matter what he said about having wanted her—and she tucked that away to pull out and think about later—the fact remained that she'd used him.

"I told you I'd been married," she began quietly. "What I didn't tell you was that I had a baby."

She heard the quick rush of Devlin sucking in his breath but she didn't lift her gaze from the bed.

"When Bill and I got married, I think we were both looking for a family more than anything else. He came from a very wealthy background. His parents had never had much time for him and I think, in his own way, he was as lonely as I was.

"We were happy. He was kind and funny and we laughed a lot." Her face softened with the memories and Devlin felt an odd little stab of something that could have been jealousy but obviously wasn't.

"We wanted to start a family right away, even though we were both pretty young ourselves. Both of us wanted children. We wanted the sort of stability and balance that a family can give. So we started trying to have a baby. Only nothing happened. After a few months, we went to a doctor and they started running tests."

She plucked at the sheet, her forehead puckering as she remembered the endless poking and probing, the intimate questions from doctors she'd never seen before and would never see again.

"They finally told us that it was my fault. That there was something wrong with my tubes and it would take surgery or a miracle for me to conceive. And even with the surgery, the miracle wouldn't hurt."

"So you had the surgery."

"No." She shook her head. "Bill and I talked about it and decided that maybe this was some sort of sign. We were so young and so earnest about life. We decided maybe we were meant to adopt children instead. I mean, I knew firsthand what it was like to be bounced from place to place, never really belonging, never having anyone you could count on. So we decided that was what we'd do."

"What happened?" he prompted her when she fell silent.

"A miracle." Her mouth curved in a smile of such beauty Devlin looked away. "I got pregnant before we had a chance to do more than just start looking into adoption. We were ecstatic. We decided to hold off on the adoption, and then, in a couple of years, we could start the process again and adopt the rest of our family.

"I had a wonderful pregnancy. It was as if all the trouble I'd had conceiving had somehow made the pregnancy go more smoothly. My labor was easy and Bill was there when Mary was born."

Unconsciously she clasped her hands over her elbows, hugging herself almost as if she were holding a child.

"She was the most perfect baby you've ever seen. She hardly ever cried. She was always laughing and happy."

She glanced at him with a self-conscious laugh. "I know all parents say that, but Mary really was special."

"I believe you," he said gently. "What happened to her, Annalise?"

Her smile faded. "She started to have problems when she was not quite a year old. It didn't seem too serious at first but we took her to the doctor. We thought we were being overanxious parents. But we weren't. The doctor told us she had Tay-Sachs disease. It's a genetic disorder. A perfectly healthy parent can be a carrier and pass it on to their child."

She was silent, staring into the middle distance, her face without expression.

"By the time Mary was two, she was blind. She died just after her third birthday."

The stark recital only added to the impact of her words. Without any breast-beating, she expressed all the terrible anguish she must have suffered.

"I'm sorry." The words were hopelessly inadequate of course, but there didn't seem to be anything else he could say.

"Thank you."

"When…I mean, how long ago…" He let his voice trail off.

"A year ago. I had her cremated and I scattered her ashes over a lake we used to visit. She liked to watch the gulls before…before she lost her vision." She had to stop to clear her throat and then she continued more briskly.

"And then I packed everything in my car and started driving. I got odd jobs here and there, but I couldn't seem to concentrate very well. I was fired a couple of times. Sometimes I just quit because I couldn't bear to be in one place for very long.

"I guess I thought if I just kept moving, the pain wouldn't find me. Only it always did."

That explained her frantic rush earlier. She hadn't been desperate for him to make love to her. She'd been desperate to try to forget. Seeing Clay had brought all the hurt rushing back over her. That's what she meant when she said she'd used him.

"Annalise, what about Bill? Where was he?"

"He left," she said simply.

"He left you and your daughter?" Devlin felt rage churn in his gut. "The son of a bitch just walked out?"

"It wasn't like that," she protested. "You mustn't think badly of him."

"Oh, mustn't I?" he muttered, wishing he had the man in front of him so he could slowly choke the life from his miserable body. He got up and stalked to the dresser, snatching a clean pair of shorts out of a drawer and stepping into them with a motion nothing short of violent. He grabbed a pair of jeans and jerked them on.

"What kind of man walks out with his wife and daughter just when they need him the most?"

"A good man." She held up one hand when he looked as if he might explode. "And a weak one, I suppose."

"You suppose?" Absently he handed her one of his shirts to replace the sheet she was still holding over her breasts. When she hesitated, he half turned away, though it seemed a bit late in the day to be worrying about modesty.

"Bill wasn't a bad person," Annalise insisted as she buttoned the soft cotton over her breasts. "He felt terribly guilty about Mary being ill. When she was diagnosed, we had tests run and found out that Bill was the one who carried the gene for Tay-Sachs. He felt as if it was his fault that she was ill."

"I can understand that," Devlin admitted grudgingly. "But I can't understand how he could leave you alone to cope with it."

"Some people just aren't strong enough to deal with something like that," she said, smoothing the tail of the shirt across her thigh. "He tried. He really did. But after a while, he couldn't even bear to look at her."

"So he dumped you?" The incredible thing was that he couldn't hear so much as a hint of bitterness in her voice, not a trace of anger.

"No. He moved out and I filed for divorce. But he continued to support us. I couldn't work, of course. Taking care of Mary was a full-time job. He paid for a house and all the medical expenses. We didn't have to worry about anything."

"Conscience money." Devlin dismissed her ex-husband's motives without hesitation.

"Maybe. But it was all he could give us."

"It wasn't enough," he snapped, angry for her.

"You can't ask more of someone than they're capable of giving," she said softly. "I don't hate him. I know he felt guilty about not being there for me, for Mary. He'd have continued to take care of me for the rest of my life if I'd wanted."

"Big deal."

Annalise didn't try to argue any further. She couldn't really expect Devlin to understand Bill. Devlin faced the world square on, dealing with whatever life threw at him. Until Mary's illness, Bill had never had to deal with anything more challenging than choosing the color of a new car.

When he'd been faced with something that would have been hard for anyone to deal with, he hadn't had the strength to stand up to it. He'd run away. It was something he'd have to live with for the rest of his life. If he deserved a punishment, that was surely more than enough.

She released a slow breath, aware that she felt incredibly tired and, simultaneously, lighter than she had in months. It was as if, in talking about what had happened, she'd shed some of the burden of the grief she'd carried for so long. She stifled a yawn.

Devlin had been pacing the room with long, restless strides as if he needed to do something to wear off the tension. Now he stopped next to where she sat on the side of the bed. Annalise looked up at him, her eyes questioning.

Hesitantly he reached out to touch his fingertips to her cheek, the tender gesture slightly awkward. She wondered if she was aware of the conflict she could read so clearly in his eyes.

After a moment, his hand dropped back to his side and he half turned away, looking out the window where the rain was still falling in a steady patter. Darkness had fallen while they talked, hurried along a bit by the storm clouds.

"I guess I ought to shut the doors, make sure I didn't leave any tools out in the rain."

"Yes." It suddenly seemed too much of an effort to hold her head up.

"Are you hungry? I could heat up some soup."

"No, thank you." She yawned again. "I'm just so tired."

"Go to sleep, then. I'm going to check on... things," he said vaguely.

Annalise watched him leave. She wanted desperately to fight the drowziness. There were things that needed to be said. But she couldn't think what they were.

Sighing, she lay down, curling up on her side, her face buried in Devlin's pillow. She'd only rest her eyes for a few minutes and then she'd be ready to cope again.

Devlin stood in the living room, staring out the window at the steady fall of rain. Ice clinked against the side of his glass as he raised it and took a swallow of its contents. He felt the Chivas slide down his throat, creating a mellow warmth in the pit of his stomach.

He rarely drank and never more than one drink. He'd had too much to drink the night Harold Sampson had murdered his wife and left all the evidence pointing in Devlin's direction. The fact that he'd admitted as much hadn't helped his defence any. But tonight, the Scotch helped ease his inner chill.

He twisted the glass in his hands, watching the amber liquid shift around the clear ice cubes. There had been moments during the past few days when he'd entertained the thought that maybe, if he slept with Annalise, it would solve a whole host of problems, enabling him to stop taking cold showers and start sleeping at night. If he could make love to her just once...

His soft laughter was self-directed and held little humor. Of all the hopeless male fantasies, that had to be one of the oldest and, apparently, one of the most enduring. Sex rarely solved more problems than it created. You would think he'd have known that.

Not that knowing it would have stopped him from making love to Annalise. Nothing short of a cataclysm of truly spectacular proportions could have stopped him once he'd felt the depth of her response.

Of course, that response hadn't been the result of anything likely to increase the size of his ego. Annalise hadn't been desperate for him to make love to her. She'd been desperate to forget, at least momentarily, the grief that gnawed at her.

Devlin's mouth twisted in a rueful smile. It wasn't the sort of thing a man liked to hear from a beautiful woman to whom he'd just made love. His smile faded and he took another swallow of Scotch.

For someone who didn't intend to get involved, he'd done a rather poor job of keeping his distance. He frowned uneasily. There was no more pretending that he didn't care about Annalise. But there was also no reason to let things get out of hand.

He'd known for a long time that he wasn't suited to deep, personal involvements. He would never marry, never have children. His frown grew brooding as he looked into a future that stretched out ahead of him like a long, lonely road.

But that was the way it had to be. There were risks you just didn't take in life. One of the ones he'd promised himself never to take was the chance of ever hurting people the way his father had. It was common knowledge that abused children grew up to become abusive parents. Not all of them certainly, but the statistics made it clear that the odds were against him.

He couldn't quite picture himself striking a woman or a child, but it wasn't a chance he was willing to take. He was capable of violence. He'd known that even before he went to prison. The years in prison had sharpened that side of him—he wouldn't have survived without it.

There were those who would argue that the situations were quite different. One was defending your life, the other was attacking a person smaller and weaker than yourself. Because he was capable of one didn't necessarily mean he was capable of the other.

But what if that edge was sharper than he knew? What if the violence was so deeply ingrained in him that it came out when he wasn't expecting it? He'd lived with violence in one form or another most of his life. You couldn't just walk away from that kind of heritage.

He downed the last of the Scotch, feeling it settle in the pit of his stomach, a smooth pool of fire that helped ease the ache.

It had been, God help him, a relief to learn that Annalise couldn't have children. Not that he wouldn't have given his right arm if it would give her back the child she'd lost. But it wouldn't be his child—never his. It was a measure of how crazed he'd been that the thought of using protection hadn't even crossed his mind. All he'd been able to think of was that he had to have her.

The truth was, he still wanted her. If he'd ever thought that his craving would be permanently eased if he had her just once, he'd been wrong. Scant hours after making love to her, he wanted her as much as if he'd never had her.

Annalise came awake slowly, aware that, while her mind was still tangled with sleep, her body tingled with life. She shifted, moaning softly as she dragged her eyes open.

The room was filled with the odd half-light that came just before dawn, all gray shadows and softened angles. She was naked, the covers stripped down to the foot of the bed, yet her body felt heavy with warmth.

Devlin knelt beside her, his eyes intent as he looked down at her. She blinked, trying to clear the sleepy fog from her vision.

"Devlin?"

He didn't seem to hear her husky whisper. His hands settled lightly on her shoulders, stroking downward until they hovered over her breasts, almost but not quite touching. From the sensitized feel of her nipples, Annalise knew it wasn't the first time he'd touched her, literally stroking her awake.

She opened her mouth to offer a shaky protest, but his palms settled on her breasts, his work-calloused thumbs brushing across the peaks, and her protest emerged as a moan.

"Devlin—" He bent and covered her mouth with his, swallowing whatever she'd planned to say. His tongue traced the line of her lower lip, coaxing her to open for him. Helpless to resist—not at all sure she even wanted to resist—Annalise parted her lips, inviting him inside.

The first time they'd made love, she'd set the pace. She'd been running from her hurt more than reaching for the pleasure she'd half sensed he could give her. This time, Devlin was in control. As the minutes stretched, it seemed as if he were not only in control of himself but in control of her.

Her body responded to his touch as if she'd been waiting for him all her life, storing up all the passion she'd thought she didn't possess so that this man could release it.

He savored the time she'd denied him earlier, alternately coaxing and commanding as he led her down pathways she'd never traveled before. His fingers knew just where to stroke her, just when to touch as lightly as a butterfly's wing and when a firmer touch would set her shivering with need.

He soothed. He demanded. He pleaded. And she gave him every trembling response he asked for.

When the time came, she opened to him eagerly, her hunger as great as his. But even now, he wouldn't allow her to rush things. He caught her face between his hands, his eyes intent on hers as he lowered his head and closed his mouth over hers, his tongue plunging deep even as his hips sank into the cradle of her thighs. His mouth swallowed her cry of pleasure.

He made love to her with fierce tenderness. She met his every thrust. Her hands moved frantically up and down his sweat-dampened back, feeling the ripple of his muscles.

Inside her, a spring coiled tighter and tighter until her whole body was tuned into that building tension, until she knew she would surely shatter into a million pieces if he continued.

And then Devlin's hand cupped her bottom, tilting her hips to receive him more fully. Annalise's breath left her in a surprised cry as the spring suddenly broke loose and sent her spinning outward. For a moment, it seemed as if her heart would stop with the intensity of it.

She felt Devlin swell inside her and felt the pulse of his release. His hands tightened almost painfully on her hips. A guttural groan tore from his throat. Annalise felt her own pleasure sharpened in the knowledge that he trembled against her.

The only sound was the rasp of Devlin's breathing. Annalise ran her hands slowly up and down his back, exploring the ridged length of his spine. He was heavy, but she liked the feel of him on her, within her.

She felt at peace in a way she couldn't remember feeling in a very long time. Maybe it was the fact that she'd told Devlin about Mary last night. Maybe it was the wonderful feeling of physical fulfillment he'd just given her.

Whatever it was, she knew deep inside that she'd finally turned a corner. She was moving out of the darkness now, moving toward the light. She'd never stop grieving for her daughter, but she'd finally accepted the need to move on.

The healing had finally begun, and she owed it to the man she held in her arms.

Chapter 9

The next time Annalise woke, the sun was pouring in through the light curtains, cutting a warm golden path across the bed. Devlin's bed.

She stretched, her mouth curving in a smile. She felt several unfamiliar, delicious aches, and her smile softened with sensuous memories. She'd always thought the writers who described sex as stars bursting overhead had rather vivid imaginations. But last night, she'd seen more than a few bursting stars herself.

She sat up, reaching for the robe Devlin had draped across the foot of the bed. Her robe, she noticed, her smile deepening. Not only was he a devastating lover, he was thoughtful, too. All in all, a pretty terrific combination.

Annalise got out of bed and shrugged into the robe, pulling her hair out from under the collar. She could smell coffee and bacon, and she was suddenly ravenously hungry.

She went into the bathroom. Her attention was caught by her reflection in the mirror, and she paused to look at herself. She looked different. Just like in the books where everyone could tell the heroine had let the hero have his wicked way with her, she could see the difference in her own face.

She looked younger. The lines of tension that had added years to her age were softened. Her eyes seemed brighter. For the first time since hearing the doctor pass sentence on her beautiful little girl, she was looking forward without a sense of dread.

It didn't matter that her place in Devlin's life was ill defined. She wasn't going to worry about the future. She'd been taking each day as it came, and the results had been worthwhile so far. More than worthwhile, she amended, thinking how short a time ago it had been that she was living in her car, beyond caring how she'd make it to the next day.

Devlin was standing at the stove when she entered the kitchen. Though she didn't make a sound, he must have felt her presence. She saw his back stiffen in the moment before he turned.

There was a certain wariness in his eyes, as if he weren't quite sure what to expect from her. Which made them even, she thought, toying with the belt on her robe. Because she didn't know what to expect, either.

"Hi." Devlin broke the silence.

"Hi."

"How are you feeling?"

"Okay."

She stared down at her bare feet, wishing she had a little more experience with this sort of thing. Was there a proper thing to say or do at a moment like this? Should she pretend nothing had happened? Or should she throw her arms around him? Something in between the two seemed a likely bet, but just what, she couldn't have said.

"Look, I—"

"I hope—"

Both broke off and looked at each other.

"You first," Devlin said.

"No, you go first. I don't know what I was going to say, anyway," she admitted with a shy smile.

There was an almost invisible easing of his shoulders. "I'm not all that sure what I was going to say, either."

"Really?"

"Really." His mouth relaxed in something approaching a smile. "I was probably going to ask you how you were again."

"I guess there aren't any firm rules on what you're supposed to say when you've just—I mean, after..." The words trailed off and she felt color come up in her cheeks.

"When you've just become lovers?" he said softly, his eyes kindling with memories. He started forward, stopping squarely in front of her.

Annalise focused her eyes on the top button of his shirt, feeling a newly familiar warmth in the pit of her stomach.

"Is that what we are?" she whispered. "Lovers?"

"Is that what you want us to be?"

She lifted her eyes to his face, seeing the question in his gaze. He was just as uncertain about this as she was, she realized suddenly. It was a novel idea. She didn't think Devlin Russell was uncertain about very many things.

"Yes." There was no hesitation in her reply.

His hands settled on her shoulders, his thumbs stroking absently across her collarbone. His expression was still serious, his eyes still held that odd wariness.

"Annalise, I'm not making any promises for the future."

"I'm not asking for any."

"There are things you don't know about me."

"I know enough."

"I don't want to see you get hurt."

Her fingers touched his mouth, silencing him. "Let the future take care of itself. I'm not asking you for anything more than you want to give, Devlin."

He closed his eyes, remembering her saying that her husband had given all he could—that you couldn't ask more of anyone than that. He'd dismissed the man as a sniveling coward. But was he really so different? Wasn't he asking Annalise to be satisfied with what he could offer?

For her own sake, he should bundle her into her car and hustle her out of his life as quickly as possible. He opened his eyes and looked at her, seeing nothing but acceptance in her gaze.

His hands tightened on her slender shoulders, drawing her closer. He knew he should send her away, but knowing and doing were two different things. He'd been alone most of his life. Would it really be so terrible to let her ease the loneliness that sometimes gnawed at him?

If he was careful, if he didn't let it go too far, maybe they could each draw something from the other. And when the time came, they could walk away without regrets. There was no harm in being a little involved.

As he bent to kiss her, he shoved aside the small voice that whispered that being a little involved was rather like being a little dead. It wasn't something you could do halfway.

If Annalise had ever thought she wasn't a particularly sensuous woman, she quickly learned how wrong she'd been. In Devlin's bed, in his arms, she found out that she had depths of sensuality she'd never expected.

If she'd been asked, she would have said that her ex-husband was a good lover. He'd certainly been kind and considerate, never demanding.

Devlin demanded. He wasn't content to have her simply lie beneath him, accepting his possessions. He demanded her participation, coaxing it from her with his hands and mouth. *His* satisfaction wasn't enough. He wasn't satisfied until he felt her skin heating beneath his hands and heard the soft cries she was helpless to suppress.

Though she tried not to, it was impossible to avoid comparing the only two lovers she'd ever had. She told herself she was being unfair. Bill had been young when they married, with little more experience than she. He'd never hurt her, never tried to coerce her into having sex if she didn't wish to. Making love with him had been a moderately pleasant if not terribly exciting act.

It was only now that she realized just how much she'd missed out on. Sex with Devlin could never be described as "moderately pleasant." It was passionate, consuming, achingly tender. He was more attuned to her body than she was, teaching her that there were more erogenous zones than the obvious ones.

She'd never have imagined that the skin behind her knees was so sensitive or that having him kiss the inside of her elbow could send shivers of awareness through her.

He encouraged her to explore his body as thoroughly as he had hers. Annalise was hesitant at first. It wasn't that she was unfamiliar with the male anatomy. After all, she had been married. But it was a long step from knowing what a man looked like without his clothes and feeling the strength of him under her hands.

But his response encouraged her to overcome her shyness. And she discovered that there was something intensely erotic at feeling Devlin tremble and knowing it was because of her. It made her feel bold and deliciously wicked.

When she thought about it, she was amazed by how quickly and easily they made the shift from roommates to lovers. Though she left most of her things in the spare bedroom, Annalise never used the bed there. It felt natural to go to sleep in Devlin's arms, wonderful to wake up in his bed.

She wondered sometimes just where they were headed. He'd said he couldn't make her any promises, told her there were things she didn't know about him. She didn't doubt he was right.

She still hadn't the faintest idea how he'd come by the kind of money he was spending on the house, especially since he never made any mention of a job he'd had in the past or might return to in the future. But she didn't really care where the money had come from.

She knew the most important things about Devlin Russell. She knew that he was kind and much softer than he'd probably willingly admit. He'd not only pulled her out of the river, he'd helped her put her life back together.

He pretended to be indifferent to Beauty and her offspring, but he never forgot to make sure there was plenty of cat food in her dish. When the kittens started leaving their home in his closet and venturing into the wide world beyond, Devlin never once showed the slightest sign of impatience at finding them constantly underfoot.

When pathetic wails emanated from the bathroom at two in the morning, Devlin was there hard on Beauty's heels. He fished one particularly daring explorer out of the empty bathtub, which had been easy enough to get into but proved impossible to escape from. Annalise watched sleepily from the bed.

"They like you," she said, cuddling up to his side as he slid under the sheet.

"They're a pain in the neck," he muttered. But the complaint lacked any real force.

She smiled in the darkness. It was funny how he always downplayed his softer side, as if it might make him vulnerable to admit it existed. But she knew it was there.

Devlin's sister showed up again a few days after her first meeting with Annalise. Devlin was in town picking up some lumber when Annalise heard the car coming up the driveway. She'd been shredding chicken for a salad. At first she thought it was Devlin returning, but the deep rumble of the truck's engine was missing.

Rinsing her hands in the sink, she pulled a towel off the rack and dried her hands as she went to the front door. She recognized the car immediately.

Color climbed her cheeks when she thought of Kelly's last visit. Devlin's sister must think she was insane. If Devlin had been home, she might have been tempted to duck out the back door rather than face Kelly again. But Devlin wasn't here and she could hardly ignore his sister.

Drawing in a deep breath, she pushed open the screen door and stepped onto the porch as Kelly crossed the yard. There was no sign of her baby and Annalise felt a twinge of relief. She knew she wouldn't fall apart again, but it would be a long time before she could look at a baby without feeling the pain of her own loss. Maybe that time would never come.

"Hello." Kelly's smile was friendly as she approached the porch.

"Hi." Annalise hoped her own smile didn't reflect her nervousness. "I'm afraid Devlin's not here."

"I figured that when I didn't see his truck." Kelly climbed the steps and stopped beside her, reaching up to take off the sunglasses that shaded her dark eyes. "Mind if I wait for him?"

"Of course not." Annalise was shocked that she felt she had to ask. She pulled open the screen. "I made some lemonade earlier today. Would you like some?"

"Sounds like heaven." Kelly followed her into the kitchen. "It looks like you were in the middle of something. Why don't you finish it and I'll pour the lemonade?"

Annalise hesitated, but Kelly was already pulling open the refrigerator.

"What are you making?"

"Sesame chicken salad." She returned to the task of stripping the chicken from its bones. "It's been so hot, I thought a salad would be nice."

"It looks like this summer is going to be a real scorcher, doesn't it? Have you been living with my brother very long?"

The question was asked in the same casual tone as her comment about the weather. It took Annalise a moment to register the change of subject.

"Not long. A few weeks."

"How long have you known him?" Kelly asked brightly. She filled two glasses with lemonade and set the pitcher down before fixing Annalise with inquiring eyes.

Annalise took her time about answering. She finished the last piece of chicken and scooped the meat into a bowl. She washed her hands and picked up the towel to dry them before turning to look at Kelly.

There was curiosity in the younger woman's eyes but no hostility. Annalise couldn't have blamed her if she'd been more than a little doubtful about her brother's houseguest, considering her performance when they'd met. But if Kelly had doubts, she was concealing them.

"Actually, I met your brother a few weeks ago," she said slowly, trying to decide how much to say. What would Devlin want his sister to know? There was no way of knowing, and since Devlin wasn't here, she was just going to have to go with her own instincts.

"I fell in the river, and he pulled me out."

Kelly's eyes widened. The glass she'd just lifted hit the table with a thump that threatened to slosh lemonade over the top.

"You're kidding."

"No." Annalise folded the towel with nervous precision and set it on the counter. She linked her hands in front of her. "I didn't have any money or anywhere to go so he let me stay here. I've been helping him with some records and doing most of the phone calls to suppliers."

"You don't have to explain to me." She stopped and gave Annalise a sheepish smile. "I suppose I more or less asked for an explanation," she admitted.

"I don't mind. I don't blame you for being curious."

"Well, I suspect Devlin wouldn't feel the same way. My big brother has a nasty habit of never telling me anything. Sometimes I think he must have been a superspy all those years he was gone."

Annalise smiled but didn't comment. She'd thought the same thing herself. She knew Devlin had left home at eighteen and that he hadn't come back to Indiana until a year ago, but he'd never mentioned what he'd done during the years in between. Just like he'd never mentioned where he'd gotten the money to build the house. But she didn't think he'd particularly appreciate her speculating about his past with his sister.

"I'm glad you came back," she said. "I wanted to apologize for my behavior the other day. I must have seemed like a crazy woman."

"No. You seemed like someone who was in pain. I've been there a time or two myself. You don't have to apologize."

Until that moment, Annalise hadn't seen much resemblance between Kelly and Devlin. But there was a certain look of acceptance in Kelly's eyes that suddenly made her think of the way Devlin had taken her in without asking questions, without demanding explanations. It was a rare quality but one the Russells seemed to have more than their share of.

"Thank you. But I want to apologize anyway. And I feel as if I should explain."

"Don't feel you have to."

"I want to." Annalise moved away from the counter to pull out a chair at the kitchen table. Kelly followed suit, sitting down across from her.

"A little over a year ago, my daughter...died."

There didn't seem to be any other way to say it, but the words sounded flat and harsh in contrast to the bright sunshine that filled the kitchen. It hurt to hear them. Saying it aloud seemed to sharpen her loss.

"How terrible." Kelly's sympathy was quick and warmly offered. "I'm so sorry."

"Thank you." Annalise gave her a shaky smile. "Mary was older than . . . your baby, but for a minute, when I saw him, it just brought it all back. But that's no reason for me to run out like such an idiot."

"Please. Don't apologize, Annalise. I can't even begin to imagine how you must feel. If something happened to Clay, I'd . . . I just don't know what I'd do." Kelly blinked against the sting of tears, unable to conceive how she'd go on if something happened to her son.

She reached across the table, her hand closing over Annalise's. Though she'd promised herself that she wasn't going to cry, Annalise felt tears fill her eyes when she met Kelly's gaze. Maybe it was the fact that Kelly had a child of her own that made her sympathy seem so personal.

"Thank you." She turned her hand, returning Kelly's grip. Her smile was shaky but hardly more so than Kelly's.

The low rumble of Devlin's truck coming up the driveway interrupted before either of them could say anything more. Annalise felt a mixture of regret and relief. There was relief in having the too-intense moment broken, regret because it seemed as if she and Kelly might have made a start toward a friendship given a little more time.

* * *

Kelly watched her older brother's arrival with interest. It had only been a few days since she'd found out that Annalise was living with him, but that had been more than enough time for her to speculate endlessly over the sudden arrival of a woman in Devlin's life.

Since a lot of her speculating had been done out loud, it had been her husband's suggestion that she drop in on Devlin again. Actually Dan's suggestion had been more of a plea. He'd taken Clay with him for the day and all but ordered her to go see her brother and satisfy her curiosity.

Kelly had been relieved when she arrived to find only Annalise. She knew from past experience that she would get little satisfaction from trying to pry information out of Devlin. Better to question the furniture, it was more likely to answer.

In the year since he'd unexpectedly appeared on her wedding day, he'd told her almost nothing of where he'd been or what he'd done in the ten years since he'd left home. She'd respected his right to privacy.

No one knew better than she what his childhood had been like. It wasn't the sort of background that encouraged a person to be open and forthcoming with other people, even with those who cared for them. The wariness in his eyes told her that the intervening years hadn't given him any reason to open up.

Kelly accepted his choice, even as she ached for the hurts that made him keep the world—including her—at a distance. She'd been completely unprepared to find that he had a woman living with him.

He'd said that Annalise was staying with him, making it sound as if she were more of a temporary boarder than anything else. Annalise had also implied that her staying with Devlin was little more than a case of him offering her a helping hand when she'd needed it.

But it didn't take more than a few moments of observing them together for Kelly to be sure that they were sharing a bed, as well as a house. It wasn't anything obvious. It was subtle things. A certain intimacy in the way they looked at each other, in the casual way Annalise straightened his shirt collar.

That Annalise cared for him was easily read in her eyes. What Devlin felt was harder to say. He didn't reveal his feelings easily. But it seemed as if there were a little less tension around his eyes, a subtle relaxation in the way he held his shoulders.

Kelly could only hope that, whatever was developing between the two of them, neither of them were going to get badly burned.

It was a few days after Kelly's second visit that the dog showed up. He was not a terribly prepossessing animal. Of a size approaching huge and a color best described as nondescript, he was shaggy, filthy and undoubtedly riddled with fleas.

The first time Annalise saw him, he was trying to tip over the trash cans. He darted off as soon as he saw her, and she thought that was the last she'd see of him. But he was back a few hours later, a gray shadow in the brush at the edge of the yard.

Her heart went out to him. He was so obviously starving. She got some hamburger from the refrigerator and put it on a plate that she carried out into the yard. The dog darted away as soon as she stepped into the yard, but she had the feeling he hadn't gone very far. She set the meat down a few yards away from the porch. She returned to the house, but lingered at the back door to see what would happen.

It wasn't long before the dog reappeared. He approached the plate warily, his eyes darting back and forth as if looking for a trap. The food disappeared so quickly, she halfway expected him to eat the plate before he realized it wasn't edible.

She'd been feeding the dog for three days before Devlin noticed. Annalise had just put out another plate of hamburger and was standing on the back porch, watching the dog eat. He'd become a little more confident, no longer running as soon as he saw her. She'd been wondering how long it would take to get him to the point where he'd let her approach him and hadn't heard Devlin's approach.

"A friend of yours?"

She jumped and spun around guiltily. Devlin stood behind her, his eyes on the dog, who'd lifted his head from the plate and was watching the two of them warily. Annalise was one thing, but Devlin was an added factor that he wasn't at all sure of.

"He was starving," she said, getting to the point immediately.

"He looks like you should be feeding him hay instead of meat," Devlin suggested, eyeing the dog's massive frame.

"He doesn't eat much." Since the dog was polishing off a pound of hamburger just then, it wasn't perhaps the most truthful thing she'd ever said.

Devlin's gaze settled on her face, his expression unreadable. "I'd guess he doesn't eat any more than a small pack of wolves."

"I couldn't let him go hungry," she said, nibbling on her lower lip.

"Don't worry about it. I'll pick up some dog food when I go into town this afternoon. Is there anything else you need?"

And that seemed to be all he had to say about the dog. He didn't offer any objections to the animal's presence, any more than he'd objected when Beauty joined his household or when her kittens had slowly taken over the house, treating it as their own personal playground.

Annalise named the dog Lobo, in honor of Devlin's comment about him eating like a pack of wolves, and invested considerable time in convincing him that she could be a friend, as well as a source of food.

Devlin showed no real interest in the latest addition to his former household of one. Annalise thought he was completely indifferent until she came home from a rare solo trip to Remembrance to find Devlin seated cross-legged in the middle of the backyard, a plate of hamburger a few feet away from him and Lobo crouched warily a little beyond it.

The house must have blocked the sound of her car from reaching Devlin. She had no doubt he wouldn't want her to know that he was trying to gain Lobo's trust. As she watched, Lobo crept a little closer to the meat, his shaggy belly dragging on the grass.

Devlin didn't move. She could hear the low rumble of his voice, though he was speaking too softly for her to make out any words. The words weren't as important as the tone. Lobo's ears pricked forward slightly, and he edged a little closer to the food.

Annalise couldn't have said how long she stood there watching, and she had no way of knowing how long Devlin had been waiting before she arrived, but he never showed a hint of impatience as Lobo slowly made his way to the food. Devlin didn't move as the dog ate, keeping up the same low-voiced conversation, which was answered by an occasional puzzled look from Lobo or a twitch of an ear.

When the plate was empty, Lobo didn't immediately dart away. Instead, he lifted his head to look at Devlin. He licked his muzzle, his eyes seeming to hold a question. Moving slowly, Devlin lifted his hand, stretching it out palm up. Lobo sniffed the air between them, and for a moment, Annalise thought he was going to take the man up on his invitation to come closer. But instead, he shook himself as if shaking away the urge to be too trusting and turned and trotted off.

She'd planned to get out of sight and pretend she hadn't seen anything of the interaction between man and dog, but Devlin turned his head suddenly, almost as if he sensed her presence. It would have been ridiculous to duck back out of sight.

Annalise pushed open the screen door as Devlin stood up. He retrieved the empty plate and walked toward her, his steps slow.

"For a minute there, I thought you had him," she said.

Devlin shrugged. "From the looks of him, I'd say he's been on his own quite a while. It isn't easy for him to trust."

Rather like himself, Annalise thought, but she didn't say as much. She took the plate from him as they entered the kitchen. She rinsed it and set it in the dishwasher, turning around in time to see one of the kittens launch a fierce attack on Devlin's shoe. Devlin bent down to pull his attacker loose from his shoelace, settling the infant in the palm of his hand, where it promptly began to chew on one of his fingers.

"You're very good with animals," she told him softly, watching him deal with the kitten.

"It doesn't take much." He deposited the kitten on the floor, where it promptly darted off in search of new mischief.

"You were very comfortable with your nephew," she added, remembering how easily he'd handled the infant, without any of the stiffness men usually showed when confronted by a baby. "You'd be a good father."

"No." The single word was flat and harsh. "That's something I'll never be."

He walked out without another word, leaving Annalise staring after him with a frown. What had she said to upset him?

* * *

Devlin strode out of the house, aware that he'd overreacted. Annalise's comment had been nothing more than the sort of casual remark anyone might make. She'd had no way of knowing that her words were going to touch a sore spot that he'd thought healed long ago.

Maybe he wouldn't have snapped at her if he hadn't suddenly had a picture of her stomach swollen with child—his child. He shook his head, dismissing the image. It was impossible for more reasons than one.

Even if Annalise could have children, she'd never have his child. No woman would ever have his baby. If there was any chance at all that the madness that had driven his father to abuse his children was buried somewhere inside him, he'd never take that risk.

There were moments when he lay awake at night, listening to Annalise's quiet breathing and thought of what it might be like to build a life with her as a permanent part of it. But he wasn't going to let himself be blinded to reality by a passing fantasy.

And reality was that he was a born loner. If only Annalise didn't make it so hard to remember that.

Chapter 10

It occurred to Annalise that there was a certain lack of justice in the fact that, though *she'd* been the one to start feeding Lobo, the first person he allowed to touch him was Devlin. Once that hurdle had been overcome, it wasn't long before the huge dog lost most of his wariness. But while he was tolerant of Annalise, he made his preference for Devlin's company quite clear.

Fortunately the dog's lack of appreciation was the only complaint she had with her life at the moment. She was living from day to day, putting the past behind her, not looking too far into the future.

Somewhere in the back of her mind was the knowledge that things couldn't continue as they were forever. She and Devlin were lovers, they were living together. Yet there'd been no mention of even the most rudimentary commitment between them. They'd simply drifted wordlessly from one stage to another, skipping more than a few stages in the middle.

But it felt right, and for now, that was enough. She'd lived with darkness for so long. Devlin had helped her bring light back into her life. Let the future take care of itself.

"Kelly called this afternoon," Annalise said as she scooped pasta salad onto her plate.

"Is everything all right?" Devlin set two glasses of iced tea on the table and took his seat.

"Yes. She called to invite you—well, us, I guess—to a party somebody is giving for her husband's firm. She said she could use a little moral support."

"Remington Construction was building a rather pricey batch of condos in Indianapolis," Devlin said.

"Maybe that's what it's for." She waited but he seemed more concerned with his dinner than with his sister's invitation. "What do you think?"

"I'm not really much of a party-goer. Unless you really wanted to go..." He let the question trail off. He looked up as he spoke, catching the fleeting look of disappointment, quickly smothered, in her blue-green eyes.

"No. Of course not. Do you want to call Kelly or should I?"

Devlin took his time in answering. He stabbed a curly noodle, frowning at it briefly before putting it in his mouth. He didn't taste the garlicky dressing that coated it.

Annalise had been living with him for over a month. She'd gone to Remembrance with him a few times, made the trip herself once or twice. Other than those trips and Kelly's two visits, she hadn't seen another person in all that time. It was hardly surprising if she had been looking forward to going somewhere.

It was different for him. He'd had more than his fair share of humanity after eight years in prison where privacy had been a nonexistent commodity. He could probably live the rest of his life without ever going to a town bigger than Remembrance.

A party with a bunch of people he didn't know and didn't want to know sounded just this side of hell. But there'd been that flash of disappointment in her eyes. She wanted to go and she couldn't go without him.

"Why don't you call and tell her we'll go?" he said slowly, knowing his conscience would nag at him if he suggested otherwise.

"Are you sure? You're not going because you think I want to go, are you?" she asked shrewdly.

"Of course not." He'd spent too many years in prison, he thought with a touch of black humor. He could lie without batting an eye. "Kelly is my sister and this sounds like something that's important to her. If she wants a little support, the least I can do is give it to her. You don't have to go if you don't want to," he added innocently.

"I don't mind. It sounds like it might be interesting." Annalise's mouth curved into a slow grin. "Actually, I really did want to go."

Devlin wondered if it was a dangerous sign to find himself wanting to lean across the table and kiss the smile from her lips.

Like Annalise, Devlin was living day to day. Unlike her, it was the way he'd had to live most of his life. Until recently, there'd never been a time when the future was more than a hazy picture in his mind.

When he was young, the future had consisted of surviving his father's unpredictable rages. After he left home, the future had started to take shape. He'd begun to think of what he might want to do with the rest of his life.

And then Harold Sampson had killed his wife and framed the last man who'd been fool enough to sleep with her for the crime. After that, there'd been no reason to think about the future. The state had his future all neatly wrapped up for quite a while to come.

Since leaving prison, he hadn't considered any further ahead than the next task on the house. He didn't know what he was going to do when the house was finished. Maybe he'd become one of those people who were forever adding onto their home, living in a constant state of construction. There were worse ways to spend your life. God knows, he knew that from personal experience.

Only recently, he'd begun to think that might not be enough. He'd started to wonder if there wasn't something else he'd like to do with his life. Of course, thanks to Harold Sampson's last minute surge of penitence, he didn't have to worry about earning a living.

But he didn't really like using the money. His distaste for it had grown rather than diminished. It didn't matter that, as Reed Hall had pointed out, it was the least the bastard had owed him. It still felt like blood money—paid for with his blood.

But as Reed had also pointed out, he had few marketable skills and eight years in prison would not make a good impression on his résumé.

He scowled at his reflection in the mirror. Why was he suddenly giving so much thought to the future? Hadn't he learned a long time ago that plans for the future were nearly always derailed long before they came to fruition?

His eyes shifted to the bathroom door which stood open a crack. Annalise's voice drifted from behind it as she sang an old John Denver tune. Her voice was sightly off key and he found his mouth curving upward as he listened to her mangle the lyrics.

He didn't really have to look any further for the reason he was thinking about the future more than he liked to admit. There was something about Annalise that made him do a lot of things he wasn't accustomed to doing. Like adopting stray animals he thought as he reached down to peel loose the kitten that had climbed his pant leg almost to the knee.

And going to parties he had no wish to attend. He deposited the kitten in front of Beauty who promptly flatted it with one paw and began giving it a thorough and unappreciated bath.

Devlin straightened his tie, his frown deepening. Sometimes, he found it difficult to remember what his life had been like before the storm that had brought

Annalise into his life. The picture seemed hazy around the edges, as if Annalise's presence had sharpened the focus somehow.

She'd switched to a show tune, humming the parts she didn't remember the words to. It felt good to be standing in his bedroom, listening to her getting ready just behind the bathroom door. A pair of kittens tumbled at his feet, doing their level best to tear each other to pieces. The scene was one of domestic tranquility.

That was what he felt. Tranquil. It wasn't something he'd known a great deal of during his lifetime. If asked, he might have said he didn't know what it felt like to be tranquil. But Annalise had brought that into his life.

"Do I look all right?"

Devlin had been so absorbed in his thoughts that he hadn't noticed her entrance until she spoke. He saw her reflection in the mirror and felt the breath leave his body.

Did she look all right? She looked like heaven, like every fantasy he'd ever had, like all the dreams he'd never let himself have. She looked like more than he could ever hope to possess.

He turned to face her, his expression carefully composed, revealing no hint of the tightness he felt in his stomach.

"I prefer your hair down," he said, reaching out to touch the sleek chignon that confined the heavy length.

"I thought it would look too casual," she said.

"It looks good this way," he said, banishing the slight hesitation from her expression. "You look really nice," he added, realizing immediately how hopelessly inadequate the comment was. "Beautiful," he amended. "You look beautiful."

"You really think so?" Her smile was at once pleased and shy. "Do you think this dress is okay?"

"It's fine."

It was more than fine. The style was deceptively simple. Sapphire blue fabric covered her from throat to knee and shoulder to wrist. But the soft fabric was so fluidly draped that it seemed to caress her body rather than simply conceal it. The skirt ended at her knee, floating softly around her long legs.

The color made her eyes seem more blue than green. Or maybe it was anticipation that made them look so bright and eager. He wished he'd thought of taking her out to dinner or a movie, rather than waiting for Kelly's invitation to make him realize that Annalise might crave something more than his company exclusively.

But taking her out to dinner made it seem as if they were dating. And dating was something you did when you were thinking about getting involved.

And of course you're not involved, his mind asked derisively. *You're only sleeping with her, you jerk. If that isn't involved, what is?*

"Ready to go?" He looked at his watch, as if concerned with the time. They had plenty of time, even considering the length of the drive ahead of them. But he didn't like the direction his thoughts were taking.

* * *

The sun was just disappearing from the sky as they reached Indianapolis. Devlin felt his hands tighten on the steering wheel and forced them to relax. He hated the feeling of being surrounded by so many people, so many buildings.

It was only for one evening, he reminded himself. He could tolerate anything for one evening.

But he wasn't so sure when he realized just where the party was being held. The developers hadn't spared any expense in giving the party. They'd rented one of the best restaurants in the city, which just happened to be on the top floor of one of the nicest hotels in the city. All thirty stories of it.

Standing in the beautifully decorated lobby, Devlin stared at the elevator, feeling beads of sweat break out on his forehead. The doors slid open, revealing a spacious, pleasantly lit elevator. All he saw were the box-like proportions and the fact that there were no windows, no way to get out once those doors slid shut.

"They're holding the elevator for us," Annalise said, starting forward.

Devlin's hesitation was imperceptible as he followed her. It was an elevator, he told himself. People got on and off elevators all the time. He couldn't spend his entire life avoiding them.

He stepped into the cubicle. Immediately his tie felt too tight. His jacket seemed to have shrunk. There was only one other couple on the elevator, but he felt as if the air were being used up too quickly, as if suffocation was only a breath away.

He was unaware of Annalise glancing at him, her eyes showing sudden concern. She'd sensed his hesitation in the lobby and attributed it to a lingering reluctance to attend the party. She knew he'd only decided to go because he felt obligated to support his sister, and perhaps he'd sensed the interest she'd tried to conceal.

But the tension she felt radiating from him couldn't be explained away as a lack of sociability. His jaw was so tight she knew he had to be grinding his teeth together. Beads of sweat dampened his forehead.

Concerned, she reached out to take his hand. His fingers closed over hers, his grip too tight. She offered no objection but only moved closer so that her shoulder brushed against his. The elevator faltered for an instant, a hardly perceptible shift in speed. Devlin's fingers tightened so crushingly that she had to bite her lip to stifle a gasp.

When the elevator came to a halt and the doors slid open, his relief was palpable. He stepped out quickly, as if half-afraid the doors might slide shut, trapping him inside again.

Kelly had been watching for their arrival and she appeared before them immediately, sweeping them off to where she and Dan were seated. In the hustle of introductions and greetings, there was certainly no chance for Annalise to consider Devlin's behavior. But in odd moments during the evening, she found her thoughts drifting to those few seconds in the elevator when his hand had clung to hers as if he were a drowning man and she were a lifeline.

The answer wasn't hard to guess. In fact, it was a wonder it hadn't occurred to her before. The house he'd helped to design provided more than a few clues. Every room was full of windows. Even the bathrooms had large expanses of frosted glass that let in light and made the room seem larger, less enclosed.

The only doors were on the bathrooms. He'd had to install a door when he'd settled her into the guest room. Most of the rooms didn't even have a doorway that would take a door. Wide arches visually expanded the space, preventing any sense of being closed in, no matter where you were.

Devlin suffered from claustrophobia. Not an uncommon problem. A lot of people had it to some degree. Devlin obviously had more than just a mild touch of it. He'd been holding on to his control with nothing but willpower. The ride up in the elevator had obviously been a short stay in hell for him.

It was a rare show of vulnerability from a man who went to great pains to show only his strong side. Annalise felt a wave of tenderness. If he'd told her how he felt, she'd have happily volunteered to walk up all thirty flights with him. But of course he wouldn't admit to being afraid of closed-in places. And he wouldn't welcome any mention of it, either.

Despite his reluctance to attend the gathering, she noticed that Devlin didn't seem out of place. He didn't exactly circulate, but he made himself pleasant where necessary. He spent some time talking to Michael Sinclair, who'd designed, not only the project whose completion was being celebrated, but also Devlin's house.

Michael's wife, Brittany, was a friend of Kelly's, and Kelly made it a point to introduce Brittany and Annalise. The three of them chatted comfortably. By the end of the evening, Annalise felt as if she'd furthered her fledgling friendship with Devlin's sister and perhaps made a start toward another friendship with Brittany Sinclair.

In all her years of being moved from one foster home to another, she'd never had a chance to build friendships. After a while, she'd stopped trying. It simply hurt too much when the time came to give them up. Talking with Brittany and Kelly, she felt a deep regret for all the years she'd done without the sort of easy camaraderie she sensed between the two of them.

It was a pleasant evening, but Annalise wasn't sorry when Devlin touched her elbow and suggested that they had a long drive ahead of them. She'd had a nice time, but it had been a long time since she'd been around so many people all at once, and she'd forgotten what an exhausting experience it could be.

She felt Devlin tense as they stopped in front of the elevator, and she bit her lip, wishing she dared to suggest that walking down thirty flights of stairs was a long-time desire of hers. The doors slid open and Devlin stepped through them with all the enthusiasm of a man facing a firing squad.

They had the elevator to themselves. The doors had barely closed when Annalise turned and wound her arms around Devlin's neck, pulling his head down to hers until their lips met.

Devlin felt his mind go blank with surprise. Though he'd always encouraged her participation in bed, this

was the first time Annalise had ever shown any hint of
sexual aggression.

And this was more than a hint. He sucked in a quiet
breath as she lowered one hand from his shoulder and
boldly cupped her fingers over the growing bulge beneath his fly. Passion exploded in the pit of his stomach.

He forgot all about his hatred of enclosed places. In
fact, he forgot where they were. His hands slid down
her back to cup her bottom, drawing her forward.
Annalise gasped. Her hand left him and she caught at
his shoulders for balance as he lifted her off her feet
to press her against his thighs, showing her just how
successful her attempt at distraction had been.

His lips slanted over hers, his tongue plunging between her lips, taking possession of her mouth the way
he longed to take possession of her body.

The elevator shuddered slightly as it arrived at the
ground floor. Devlin's hands released her reluctantly,
letting her feet touch the carpeted floor just as the
door slid open.

Annalise stared up at him, her eyes dazed. Her im-
pulsive attempt to distract him from his surroundings
had been so successful she'd very nearly forgotten
where they were.

"Shall we?" he murmured when she showed no
signs of moving.

"Shall we what?" She sounded as dazed as she felt.
Devlin's mouth curved in a smile, his eyes gleaming
with purely masculine satisfaction.

"Go." He turned her in the direction of the doors
and gave her a gentle push.

Neither of them said a word during the drive home. Not by so much as a word or a glance did either acknowledge those torrid moments in the elevator. They might have been completely unaware of each other.

But that wasn't the case. Annalise could feel the tension that hummed between them like a tautly pulled wire. If she'd thought the fire that had been ignited would die out during the long drive, she realized how wrong she'd been.

She didn't have to touch Devlin or even look at him to be acutely aware of him. He didn't have to put his hands on her to make her skin tingle with awareness. There was only one way for the evening to end, and the anticipation was the most arousing kind of foreplay. Proof positive that the mind was the most powerful erogenous zone.

By the time he stopped the truck beside the house, she wasn't sure her knees would support her. Devlin shut off the engine and thrust open his door without a word. Annalise pushed open her own door, but before she could slide to the ground, Devlin was there, his hands circling her waist. He lifted her easily to the ground.

Annalise had to lock her knees to keep from simply collapsing at his feet. But even that didn't help when he slammed her door shut and then crowded her back against the truck.

"Do you know how much I want you?" he whispered raggedly.

If she hadn't already guessed, she would have now. Caught between the cool surface of the truck and the heat of his body, she could feel his arousal pressed against her stomach.

"All I could think about all the way home was how much I wanted to be inside you, feeling you close around me, all hot and damp."

She bit her lip to hold back a whimper of need, closing her eyes against the glittering intensity of his. His hands slid up from her waist to cup the weight of her breasts, his thumbs brushing over her nipples, bringing them to full arousal beneath the thin fabric of her dress.

Momentarily satisfied with her reaction, he shifted his attention to her hair, his fingers searching for and disposing of the pins that held it in place. It tumbled over his forearms in a heavy silk curtain. He buried his fingers in it, tilting her head up until his mouth could find hers in a quick, hard kiss.

He bent suddenly, lifting her in his arms with a movement so full of urgency that Annalise felt her breath stolen from her. Lobo lifted his head from his paws to watch them from the corner of the porch he'd claimed as his, but he seemed to sense that this was not a time to draw attention to himself.

They were barely inside the front door before Devlin was letting her slide to her feet, his fingers searching for the zipper at the back of her dress even as his mouth closed over hers.

Passion spiraled between them at a dizzying speed. The dress fell to the floor and he lifted her, arching her back over his arm so that her breasts were thrust upward. Annalise caught her breath on a sob as his mouth closed over her. He sucked strongly at her nipple. She felt the pressure deep inside, a hot liquid pool in the pit of her stomach.

Her fingers wound in his thick, dark hair, holding him to her as he switched his attention to her other breast. She twisted against him, seeking relief for the throbbing ache between her thighs.

She was only vaguely aware that he was moving, carrying her easily, never ceasing the sweet torment of his mouth on her breasts. By the time he at last allowed her to slide slowly the length of his body, she didn't have the strength to do more than cling to his shoulders. He eased her back and down. It wasn't until she felt the bed beneath her that she realized he'd brought her into the bedroom.

"My God, Annalise!" The words were torn from him as he realized for the first time that she was wearing nothing but a pair of scandalously small blue panties and a matching lacy garter belt that held up a pair of sheer stockings.

Seeing his stunned expression, she stretched, drawing up one leg and arching her back. For the second time that night she saw beads of sweat dampen his forehead, but for a very different reason this time.

"Do you like them?" she asked him, her voice husky and seductive. She'd felt deliciously naughty when she bought them and positively wicked when she put them on. Now she felt all woman, a temptress in sapphire silk.

"Like them?" He licked suddenly dry lips. "If I'd know you had them on, I'd have been hard all night," he admitted.

"I bought them just for you." She ran the toes of one foot down his leg. "Is that a gun in your pocket or are you happy to see me?" As a Mae West imitator, she wasn't likely to make it professionally. But Devlin didn't seem to care.

"I'm *very* happy to see you," he said with a husky laugh.

He disposed of his clothes in record time, popping several buttons from his shirt when they refused to yield to his shaking fingers. Annalise felt her body flush in anticipation as the last of his clothes hit the floor, revealing the magnificent strength of his arousal.

She reached her arms up to him, needing to feel him against her. She needed to feel him inside her, driving away the emptiness. Not just the physical emptiness but the emotional hollowness that only he could fill.

At the sight of her reaching for him, Devlin felt his pulse pound in his temples, batoning at all rational thought beyond the primal need to feel her beneath him, to feel her holding him.

His need was too great to allow time for dealing with anything as complex as garters. The delicate silk panties tore. Annalise didn't care. Her need was as deep as his.

Her fingers clung to his shoulders as he came down to her, his hips wedging her legs apart. He entered her with one smooth, hard thrust, burying his aching flesh in the damp heat of her.

She cried out as the deep ache in her was at once eased and sharpened. It wasn't enough. It couldn't ever be enough. She lifted her legs to take him deeper, wanting—needing—to feel him in every fiber of her being.

The feel of her long legs, still sheathed in the thin nylon stockings, pressed against his hips made Devlin groan. He surged heavily against her, feeling her nails dig into his shoulders as she met his every thrust, her breathing coming in deep sobbing gasps.

It was too intense to last very long. Devlin felt the delicate tightening of her body around him. He struggled to hold off his own climax, wanting it to last forever. But feeling Annalise shudder beneath him, hearing her call his name at the height of her pleasure, he felt himself dragged headlong into the vortex of her peak.

Annalise felt Devlin swell even larger inside her and then a guttural cry was torn from him. She clung to him, letting his shuddering completion drive her higher still until nothing existed in the universe but the two of them.

Devlin's body was heavy on hers, but it was a welcome weight. She'd never felt as complete in her life as she did when she held him in her arms. His breathing was still ragged when he moved to relieve her of his weight. She murmured a sleepy protest and clung to him.

"I'll crush you, sweetheart." The only time he used endearments was when they were in bed, another small intimacy that she savored. Reluctantly she loosened her arms, allowing him to ease to the side.

"You realize, of course, that you could have caused me permanent physical damage," he said conversationally. He slid his arm under her shoulders and drew her closer, tangling his fingers in her hair.

"What did I do?" She rubbed her hand over his muscled chest.

"Kissing me like that in the elevator," he reproached her huskily. "Especially when there wasn't anything I could do about it until I got you home."

"Gee, I'll try not to do it again."

"Things like that can do permanent damage to a guy." Since he was carefully arranging her hair across her breast as he spoke, his fingers lingering on the tender peak of her nipple, Annalise didn't think he was too upset.

"I'm sorry," she whispered, her back arching in an unconscious invitation as he stroked his thumb over her. She'd never have believed she could feel arousal so soon after the soul-shattering lovemaking they'd just experienced.

"I suppose I could be persuaded to forgive you," he said softly. He shifted so that he was leaning on one elbow next to her, his shoulders blocking out the dim light.

"You could?" Her voice was little more than a whisper as his fingers trailed across her stomach to find the lacy waistband of the garter belt.

"But it would take some pretty powerful persuasion," he warned her.

His mouth closed over hers, muffling the soft moan that suggested she was willing to be as persuasive as he liked.

Chapter 11

It was a scorchingly hot summer day when Reed Hall's rental car rumbled down the driveway. Annalise had spent the morning pulling weeds from the small flower bed she'd put in on the curve at the end of the driveway, but the heat had driven her to retreat to the shade afforded by the porch.

Devlin had invested in a glider to supplement the lawn chair that had been the porch's only furnishing. Annalise settled into its cushioned comfort, drawing one leg up under her, leaving the toe of her other foot on the floor to keep the glider in motion.

Beauty had joined her after directing a token hiss in Lobo's direction, a gesture that was greeted with magnificent indifference by the big dog. Annalise had worried about his reaction to Beauty and her kittens, but it had proved a groundless concern.

Lobo, for all his dangerous looks, had proved to be endlessly tolerant of assorted kitten-launched attacks. In that respect, he reminded Annalise irresistibly of Devlin, hiding a marshmallow-soft interior behind a forbidding exterior.

The heat had a somnolent effect. She was drowsily contemplating whether or not to expend the energy required to go into the house and stretch out on the bed when she heard a car turn off the road onto the lane.

Devlin had been hanging drywall in the living room, but the sound of the car drew him out onto the porch.

"Are you expecting anyone?" Annalise asked him, sitting up to watch the dust-covered sedan approach.

"No." He narrowed his eyes against the bright sun.

The man who slid out from behind the wheel nearly matched Devlin's six feet two inches, but any resemblance ended there. The sun caught in hair of such a pale blond it approached white. Where Devlin was broad shouldered and solid, this man was slender, though the casual knit shirt revealed the taut ripple of muscles in his arms. He moved with an easy grace that made Annalise think of athletes she'd seen on television.

"Reed." Devlin said the name under his breath. Annalise drew her eyes from the newcomer and looked up at him. As usual, it was impossible to read his expression, although she thought there was a certain tension in his shoulders that suggested the visitor was not entirely welcome.

"A friend of yours?"

"More or less." But he didn't move forward to greet the man. Reed crossed the yard, stopping at the foot of the steps, his head tilted to look up at Devlin.

"I was in the neighborhood. Hope you don't mind."

His voice was deep and slow, with the merest trace of a drawl to hint at a Southern background.

"Reed." For a moment, Devlin didn't seem to have anything to say beyond the flat greeting. Annalise's eyes darted between the two men, wondering just what a "more or less" friend was.

"It's good to see you," Devlin said at last. He stepped forward, extending his hand.

Reed's lean face features relaxed in a smile. He climbed the steps and took Devlin's hand, shaking it with unmistakable warmth.

"It's good to see you, Devlin. You're looking good."

"Well, I pretty well had to look better than I did the last time you saw me," Devlin said, his mouth twisting with a bitter humor Annalise didn't understand.

Before Reed could respond, Devlin turned to draw Annalise into the picture.

"Annalise, this is Reed Hall, a . . . friend of mine." The hesitation before the word *friend* did not go unnoticed by Reed, but he didn't seem disturbed. "Reed, this is Annalise St. John. She's staying with me."

Not, "She's living with me." Annalise noticed how he avoided making her presence seem too permanent. She swallowed the twinge of disappointment she felt and stood up.

"I didn't realize Devlin had such good taste," Reed said with an easy smile.

"Thank you." Up close, she realized that his eyes were an unusual shade of pure green, without the slightest hint of gold. The combination of that pale hair and brilliant eyes was striking.

"I made some lemonade earlier," she said as she withdrew her hand from his. "Would you like some?"

"Sounds wonderful. I was beginning to think I should have bought a canteen in the last town."

Annalise wondered just how good a friend Devlin considered Reed. Certainly he'd never mentioned the man to her. But then, though she thought they'd attained a certain closeness these past weeks, there was still a big part of himself that Devlin kept walled off. Most of his past was behind that wall.

Considering his rather wary greeting when Reed showed up, Annalise was surprised when Devlin invited the other man to use the spare bedroom, especially since he must have known that it meant she'd have to move her clothing and few personal possessions into the master bedroom. They might have been sharing a bed for weeks, but he'd never suggested that she move her belongings into his bedroom and she hadn't mentioned it.

While Devlin and Reed were talking, she excused herself and hastily gathered her clothing from the spare bedroom and deposited it on Devlin's bed.

There was no chance to discuss the move with Devlin until just before dinner when Reed took his suitcase into his room to clean up before the meal.

Devlin was slicing vegetables for a tossed salad while Annalise kept an eye on the marinated chicken she'd slipped into the broiler.

"I put my things in your room," she said. "I assumed that was what you wanted." She slid him a questioning look, wondering if he was going to feel that she'd stepped across that invisible barrier he kept around himself.

"Sure. Clear whatever closet and drawer space you need."

Devlin sliced a cucumber with quick, sure strokes. Reed's unexpected visit had given him the excuse he needed to get Annalise moved into his bedroom. She shared his bed, but every morning she disappeared into the other bedroom to shower and dress.

At first, he'd thought it the perfect arrangement. It kept the true nature of their relationship perfectly clear. They were lovers but they weren't seriously involved. This was only a temporary arrangement for both of them, a chance to heal a few old wounds before moving on.

But lately, he'd started to realize that sharing a bed but not a bedroom was nothing more than a smoke screen he'd put up to try to convince himself of the ephemeral nature of their involvement. The fact was, he was more deeply involved with Annalise St. John than he'd ever expected, or wanted, to be with a woman. And he could debate the wisdom of that involvement from now till doomsday, but it wasn't going to change the reality of it.

As long as they *were* involved, he didn't want her sneaking out of his room to go to hers to shower and dress. Of course, he could have just suggested that she move her things into his room. But that might imply a commitment he wouldn't—couldn't—make.

Reed's visit had given him the perfect opportunity to get Annalise to move into his room without getting into a discussion of what the move *really* meant.

God, when had he become such a manipulative bastard?

He brought the knife down with too much force, causing it to slip sideways on the cutting board and nick the base of his thumb.

"Damn!" He lifted the injured hand to his mouth.

"Are you hurt?" Annalise darted to him, taking hold of his wrist to examine the injury.

"It's not bad."

"It should have a bandage. Here, rinse it off and I'll get the peroxide." Without waiting for his consent, she turned on the cold-water tap and thrust his hand under it.

With the cold water rushing over his hand, Devlin watched her rummage in the cupboard next to the sink, searching for the bottle of hydrogen peroxide and a box of adhesive strips. There was a small, concerned frown pleating her forehead. She was worried about him.

The thought flowed over him like a warm sunshine. In his life, there'd been few people who ever worried about him. His mother had never quite come into the real world long enough to worry about anyone but herself. And his father's only concern had been beating all traces of sin out of him.

Kelly cared enough to worry about him. Other than his sister, the only name that came to mind was Reed's. And even that had been largely because it was his job to worry about his client.

But Annalise wasn't his sister and she wasn't his lawyer. She wasn't bound by familial or professional obligations to be concerned. She just was.

"Here." She turned from the cupboard and shut off the water. Wrapping his hand in a soft cotton towel, she dried it gently. Devlin found himself regretting that it was such a minor cut. It seemed a pity for her to expend all that sweet concern on anything less than arterial bleeding. She examined the small cut, her frown easing.

"It really isn't too bad. Here, this may sting a little." She poured the hydrogen peroxide over the cut, lifting anxious eyes to his face as the liquid foamed into the injury.

"Waiting to see me writhe in agony?" His mouth quirked with humor.

"I just don't like hurting people, even in a good cause." She picked up an adhesive strip and opened it. "I always hated it when Mary injured herself. Sometimes, it was all I could do to keep from crying more than she did."

It was the first time he'd heard her mention her daughter since the night she'd told him about the child. She placed the strip across the cut, pressing the adhesive portion to his hand before lifting her eyes to his face again.

"I haven't thought about that in a long time," she said slowly. "It doesn't seem to hurt as much to think about her anymore. I guess maybe time really does heal all wounds.''

"I guess so." Devlin lifted his newly bandaged hand to brush a lock of hair back from her face, his fingers lingering on her cheek. He wished suddenly that time could heal the wounds that had eaten into his soul, that he could believe the time would come when he'd feel whole, when he might be able to offer her something more than what he was now.

"Are you aware that you have a small squad of furred terrorists living in your house?" Reed's question preceded him. Devlin's hand dropped away from Annalise's face and he stepped back.

When Reed stepped on the other side of the breakfast bar, he had a gray kitten in his hand, one long finger rubbing absently between its ears.

"I should have warned you about them," Annalise said, when Devlin didn't seem to have a response. "They're at the mischievous age."

"Mischievous? After climbing my pant leg—while I was still in the pants, I'd like to point out—he proceeded to launch a vicious attack on one of my shoelaces."

"Yes. Well, we haven't quite managed to convince them that shoelaces aren't alien invaders." Annalise pulled the chicken out of the broiler and poked it experimentally. "I think supper's about ready."

Reed turned out to be a pleasant and undemanding guest. He was a lawyer. He'd been working as a court-appointed defender for the past ten years. He'd taken a few months off just to drive around the country, see all the sights he'd never had time to look at.

Annalise learned more from watching him than she did from what he said. He was easygoing, regarding the world with a sort of sleepy amusement. But after a day or two, she began to get the feeling that there were a lot of things Reed kept hidden, depths he shielded with a friendly smile and an easy laugh.

When she asked Devlin how he and Reed had met, he said only that they'd met quite a few years ago but hadn't really seen all that much of each other. He didn't volunteer any more information and she didn't try to pry it out of him, not that prying would have done her much good.

Reed didn't expect to be entertained. In fact, the first day he was there, he pitched in and helped Devlin put up drywall. He freely admitted that his experience as a handyman was limited to the ability to plug in a microwave oven and occasionally pump his own gas, but he wasn't afraid to get his hands dirty, and he didn't mind asking questions until he understood what had to be done.

Devlin would have sworn that the last thing he wanted was someone working with him. One of the joys in doing so much of the work himself was that it meant long, uninterrupted hours of solitude. But Reed proved to be an undemanding companion.

Their acquaintance over the past ten years had been brief, if eventful. Despite the fact that Devlin was willing to count Reed as one of the few people to whom he could apply the word *friend*, he couldn't really say that they knew each other well.

There hadn't been time to get to know each other well. When a man was on trial for first-degree murder, he was inclined to develop an immediate intimacy with the lawyer who was defending him.

When he'd been released from prison, there'd been the pressure of deciding what to do with his sudden, unwelcome inheritance. But there'd been more time for getting to know Reed as a man rather than simply as a lawyer.

Now, seeing Reed outside his familiar element, Devlin was able to confirm the fact that he liked the man. Reed appreciated the value of silence. If he didn't know how to do something, he watched Devlin until he figured it out. In fact, it was not unpleasant to share the labor with someone.

The small, oddly matched group rubbed along quite well together for nearly a week. Annalise had settled into Devlin's bedroom so easily it was sometimes difficult to remember that she hadn't always been there. She liked seeing her rather sparse wardrobe hanging next to Devlin's shirts.

Though she'd purchased a few things with the salary Devlin paid her, she'd put most of the money in an envelope she kept under her lingerie. Most of the time, she managed to pretend that things weren't going to change, that she was just going to continue living with Devlin, growing closer to him, gaining his trust.

But reality was something Annalise had learned to live with at an early age. And she couldn't completely overlook the possibility that, sooner or later, Devlin was going to want his house to himself.

If and when that time came, she was going to need the money she was carefully putting away now. Not that he'd throw her out into the metaphorical cold, but pride demanded that she be able to leave with some dignity. Even if she had severe doubts about whether or not she was earning the salary he was paying her, at least she had some claim to the money.

Her fingers lingered on the sleeve of the jacket Devlin had worn to the party in Indianapolis. Her cheeks warmed with memories of how that evening had ended. If she left, she'd take more than money with her.

Annalise shut the closet. Time enough to think about leaving if and when the time came. At the moment, she needed to check on dinner.

Dinner was a more lively affair since Reed's arrival. He was an amusing raconteur and his years of working in criminal justice had given him a better-than-average store of anecdotes.

Tonight he had Annalise laughing over the story of a drug dealer who'd shot a man for kicking the bumper of the dealer's Cadillac and then tried to claim it was self-defence because the car was like a part of him. The man had survived and the dealer had gone to jail, still protesting with apparent sincerity that his sentence was a gross miscarriage of justice. The absurd story even managed to draw a laugh out of Devlin.

But his smile vanished with Reed's next words.

"Cases like that are what help you keep your sanity," he said, pushing his empty plate away and tilting his chair back. "Thank God, all of them aren't like yours, Devlin."

Annalise's head jerked up, her eyes darting from Reed to Devlin. "Your case?" she questioned. "Reed defended you?"

"Damn." The front legs of Reed's chair hit the floor with a thunk. His eyes sought out Devlin's. "I'm sorry."

"It's okay." But Devlin's expression said it was far from okay. He looked at Annalise, his eyes shuttered. "Reed defended me."

Annalise bit her lip, swallowing the questions bubbling up in her throat. It was obvious that he didn't want to talk about it.

"I spent eight years in prison," Devlin said abruptly, shoving back his chair and standing up.

"Eight years?" Annalise couldn't prevent the startled exclamation or the question that followed. "What for?"

"First-degree murder." The words were flat. Without another word, he turned and walked out of the kitchen. The screen door banged shut behind him as he strode out into the gathering dusk.

He left a strained silence behind him. Annalise stared at the chair he'd been sitting in, trying to absorb the impact of this new information. Devlin had spent eight years in prison for murder. That was why he never talked about the years after he'd left home.

"Me and my big mouth." Reed broke the silence, his voice rough with regret. "I assumed you'd know."

"No." She shook her head slowly. "I didn't know. Devlin doesn't talk about himself very much."

"I remember. It made him difficult to defend. I couldn't get anything out of him that would let me play on the jury's sympathies."

"What happened?" She looked at him, her eyes full of questions.

Reed hesitated and then slowly shook his head. "I've already said too much. Let Devlin tell you whatever he feels is right."

Annalise nodded. Of course he was right. It wasn't fair to go behind Devlin's back. And if Devlin chose to tell her nothing? Well, she'd live with that. It wasn't as if it really mattered. Knowing he'd been in prison didn't change him from the man she'd been living with—the man she was very much afraid she was falling in love with.

"The one thing I will tell you is that he was innocent," Reed said.

"Of course." The look she threw him said that he didn't have to bother stating the obvious.

Reed watched her as she got up and began clearing the table. He wondered if Devlin had any idea just how lucky he'd been to find a woman like Annalise.

Devlin still hadn't returned at ten o'clock. Reed had disappeared into the guest room early in the evening, commenting that he wasn't likely to be high on Devlin's list of people he was anxious to see. Annalise had stayed up, pretending to read a book.

But her mind couldn't focus on the printed page. She kept thinking about Devlin, how bleak his face had looked in those moments before he walked out.

Did he think she'd turn away from him now that she knew about his time in prison? Did he even care?

At ten-thirty, she gave up and went to bed. She knew she wouldn't sleep, but maybe it would be better if she didn't blatantly wait up for Devlin.

She'd been absolutely sure that sleep would be impossible, but she'd been unusually tired lately and she drifted off not long after climbing between the sheets.

Annalise didn't know what time it was when she woke to the sound of thunder rumbling overhead. The weather report had been promising a storm for the following day. From the sounds of it, it had arrived early. She turned sleepily, reaching out for Devlin, but the bed was empty, the sheets cool.

Memories of the evening's events swept over her and she sat up, pushing the heavy weight of her hair back from her face. A glance at the clock told her it was a little after midnight. She was just about to swing her feet out of bed and go looking for Devlin, even if it meant trekking through the fields with a flashlight when she saw the still figure at the window.

She sagged with relief. He was home and safe. Nothing else was as important as that.

She started to go to him and then hesitated. The set of his shoulders suggested that he wasn't in the mood for company. Maybe she should lie back down and pretend she hadn't wakened. But he looked so completely alone.

She slid off the bed and padded silently toward him. Lightning flashed as she stopped next to him. Thunder rumbled on its heels. He'd taken off his shirt and draped it over a chair.

"Hi," she said softly. The muscles in his back tensed as if expecting a blow.

"Go back to bed, Annalise." There was no anger in the words. There was no emotion at all in them.

"Only if you come to bed, too."

"Later."

"Then I'll stay up with you."

He shrugged as if it were a matter of complete indifference.

Annalise hesitated. In the weeks she'd lived with him, the one unspoken rule had been that neither had invaded the other's privacy. He hadn't pushed her to tell him about losing Mary, and she hadn't pushed him to tell her about the past he so carefully avoided mentioning. If she followed that pattern, then she'd go back to bed and leave him alone.

But no one should be so completely alone. She'd felt that way after losing her child. There'd been no one she could turn to to share her grief, no one who cared whether or not she lived or died. Eventually it had nearly ceased to matter to her.

She slid her arms around Devlin's waist, pressing her cheeks against the warm skin of his back. He stiffened and she thought he might pull away.

"It doesn't matter, you know," she said softly. "You don't have to talk about it, but I want you to know that it doesn't matter."

"Doesn't it?" He remained rigid in the circle of her arms, but he didn't pull away. "I spent eight years in prison. Doesn't that worry you?"

"You were innocent."

"Did Reed tell you that?"

"He didn't have to. And if you did kill someone, I'm sure you had a reason."

Her calm assumption of his innocence flowed over Devlin like a sweet benediction. His short laugh held pain.

"I could have used twelve people like you on the jury."

"Obviously, they were twelve very foolish people," she said lightly.

He turned suddenly, putting his arms around her and crushing her close. "Thank you."

"You don't have to thank me for having good sense." She rubbed her cheek against the mat of hair on his chest, saving the feel of him safe and warm in her arms.

She loved him. The thought slipped into her consciousness with hardly a ripple. It was as if it had been there all along, just waiting for her to notice it. How could she not love him?

Devlin's hand slid into her hair, tilting her head back. His eyes glittered down at her, their expression impossible to see. Lightning flashed behind him, and it occurred to her how many significant moments in their relationship had been played out with a storm as a backdrop.

"I have never in my life known anyone like you," he said, his voice hardly above a whisper.

"That makes us even, because I've never known anyone like you."

He bent to kiss her, his mouth gentle. In the kiss, he tried to express all the things he couldn't find the words to say—how much it meant to him that she believed in him, the serenity she'd brought to his life.

Annalise felt the sting of tears, and she closed her eyes to conceal them from him. She wanted to tell him she loved him, that he'd made her life whole again, that she'd always believe him.

But now was not the time. Devlin wasn't ready to hear those words from her—might never be ready.

The eastern sky was just starting to turn gray when Devlin left Annalise sleeping in the bedroom. He hadn't slept. His thoughts were too jumbled to allow him to relax.

Annalise's unquestioning belief in his innocence had affected him more than he wanted to admit. He couldn't remember anyone ever having that sort of faith in him. It made him feel strong, humble and vulnerable. It was the feeling of vulnerability that made him frown.

"If you're anticipating the need to throw me out on my ear, I'll go without a fight."

Startled, Devlin turned toward the dry voice, making out Reed's figure standing beside one of the windows.

"I was going to go on my own," Reed continued, "but I'd be happy to give you the pleasure of tossing me down the steps."

Devlin lifted his shoulders in an easy shrug as he walked forward, taking up a position on the opposite side of the window.

"I wasn't thinking about throwing you out."

"You should. I'm sorry for speaking out of turn last night." Reed offered the apology with simple sincerity.

"It's okay."

"No, it's not. I just assumed Annalise would know."

"Yeah. I hadn't gotten around to telling her." Devlin watched a thin gold edge appear on the eastern horizon. He hadn't planned on ever telling her, but there was no need to confide that to Reed. "No harm done."

"Good." Reed moved to perch on the back of the sofa. "But I'll be leaving today, anyway."

"You don't have to do that." Devlin glanced at the other man.

"Thanks. But it's time I was moving on."

Devlin didn't argue. He'd enjoyed Reed's company, but he wouldn't be completely sorry to see him go. He missed the easy space of evenings spent with no one but Annalise for company. It occurred to him that he didn't feel similar nostalgia for the many evenings he'd spent alone before Annalise's entry into his life. He pushed the thought aside.

"Why did you come?" he asked Reed. The question had been in the back of his mind ever since the lawyer's arrival.

Reed smiled, his teeth gleaming white in the near darkness. "I've asked myself that a few times."

"Did you come up with an answer?"

Reed shrugged. "I guess I needed to see that you were making out okay."

"Why wouldn't I be?"

"No reason." He shrugged again. "In the years I've worked as a public defender, I haven't had very many cases that had happy endings. The ones who get off, more often than not, are back in court before long. The ones who do time usually get out and get in trouble again. It's not a really encouraging line of work."

"Why stay with it?" Devlin leaned his shoulder against the wall, his eyes on Reed's face.

"For the few times when you know justice really has prevailed," Reed told him. "For the times when the client is innocent and you can prove it and you know they're going to stay clean." He stopped, his eyes bleak in the growing light. "But there don't seem to be very many cases like that anymore."

"So quit."

Reed's gaze jerked to his, his lean features breaking into a slow smile. "Actually, I have." The smile faded. "I've been thinking about it for a while. I had a case—" He broke off, shaking his head. "A nineteen-year-old kid. He was arrested on drug charges. He'd never been in trouble in his life."

"Was he guilty?"

"I don't think so. He said a friend of his must have left the drugs in his car. I believed him. Even if the judge didn't agree, it would have been a first offense and I could have gotten him off with nothing but probation. But just the arrest was enough to kill his chances of getting the basketball scholarship he'd been counting on to get him into college."

Reed stopped, his gaze focused on something only he could see.

"What happened?" Devlin prompted. He could guess what had happened, but he sensed that the other man needed to finish the story.

"He hung himself the night before the hearing," Reed said without emotion.

"It wasn't your fault," Devlin said after a moment.

"No. No, I know it wasn't my fault." He gave a quick half smile. "I told him he'd get probation at worst. I didn't quit because I believed Todd's death was my fault. I quit because I can't do it anymore."

"What are you going to do now?"

"I don't know." Reed hesitated a minute and then looked at him with a self-conscious grin. "Would you believe, I'm giving serious consideration to buying a ranch in Montana or Wyoming?"

"Sounds good." Devlin thought about how working to build something strong and lasting had helped heal his wounds. Maybe it could do the same for Reed.

Reed stood and stretched. "Well, I'm going to try and catch a couple hours sleep before I pack."

"You don't have to go," Devlin told him again.

"It's time. Wasn't it Ben Franklin who said that guests and fish both stink after three days? I've been here five and I think I'm beginning to detect a slight odor."

Devlin returned his grin, though he didn't argue. Reed turned toward the guest room, then he hesitated, turning back to look at his host.

"You've got one terrific lady in there," he said, nodding toward the master bedroom.

Devlin's smile faded, his expression suddenly wary. "It isn't exactly that kind of relationship," he said.

Reed's brows rose but, wisely, he didn't argue. "Well, whatever kind of relationship it is, you're damned lucky."

Devlin watched as he entered the spare bedroom. He continued to stare at the closed door, a frown tugging at his forehead. "Whatever kind of relationship it is." That was a damned good question.

Annalise reached out to take the hand Reed offered, her smile reflecting her regret at this goodbye. She liked Reed Hall. He was easy to like, but even without that, she liked the fact that he cared about Devlin.

Devlin had given her the bare outline of what had happened eight years ago, of how Reed had believed in him then. As far as she was concerned, that alone was reason enough to like the man.

"I enjoyed meeting you," she said. She wanted to say something about seeing him again someday. But her own relationship with Devlin was too uncertain. She didn't know how likely it was that she'd be here if Reed ever visited again.

"It was a great pleasure to meet you," he said, his soft drawl giving the words a courtly sound. His hand tightened over hers, his eyes taking on a serious edge.

"Have patience with him," he said abruptly, almost as if he'd read the doubts she hadn't voiced. "He's worth the effort."

Without waiting for her to come up with a reply, he bent to kiss her cheek. He released her hand, gave her a quick grin and disappeared out the door.

Annalise stared after him, listening to him exchanging a final few words with Devlin on the porch.

Have patience with him, he'd said.

She had all the patience in the world. The question was, would it do her any good?

Chapter 12

Devlin would have been happier if he could have defined Annalise's place in his life. He had to admit she had one. They were living together. When he looked around, he saw signs of her presence everywhere: a poster of a forest glade she'd tacked to two studs in the half that was drywalled living room; bright yellow curtains in the kitchen; flowers in the yard.

She'd made an impact in his life that went deeper than just sharing his bed. He'd smiled more, laughed more in the weeks she'd lived with him than he had in the ten years that had gone before.

She'd trusted him enough to share her grief, something more difficult than sharing his bed. She'd believed in him, asking no explanations. He'd told her the whole truth surrounding his conviction, holding back nothing. He hadn't killed Laura Sampson but he'd slept with her, knowing perfectly well that she was married. Annalise's eyes had offered no judgment, no reproach.

Life had left Devlin wary. Trust was something that he gave to very few people. He'd known most of his life that he'd never marry, never have children, never get deeply involved with a woman.

Yet here he was, involved with Annalise St. John, a woman who'd had more than her share of pain in life. He didn't want to add to that pain. He didn't love her, but he'd come to care for her. Yes, that was a good way to describe it. He *cared* for her.

That admission made it possible for him to admit that he'd begun to think it might be possible to have her in his life, perhaps for a long time to come.

It was all very logical. She needed a home. He had a home to offer. They got along, in and out of bed. When he thought about spending the next few years with her, it sounded like a good idea.

He couldn't offer her a grand, romantic passion. He didn't have that to offer. But he could give her security. Not marriage. He could offer everything but marriage. But she'd been that route once and he doubted she'd be interested in giving it another try.

And no children. He ached for the pain she'd suffered when she found she couldn't have children, but he couldn't pretend that he hadn't been relieved to know that was one thing he wouldn't have to worry about. And having lost her little girl, she wouldn't want to take that risk again, anyway.

She had plenty of reasons to want a gentler, more comfortable future. Maybe, just maybe, they could build that future together.

Annalise also thought a lot about the future in the days following Reed's departure. Her realization that she loved Devlin had changed everything.

After losing Mary, she'd never thought she'd be able to care deeply for another human being. The pain had been so terrible, it had been like acid eating into her soul. She'd never wanted to risk that kind of hurt again.

Devlin had proved how wrong she'd been. She'd cared for her first husband—thought she loved him. She saw now that what she'd felt for Bill had been nothing more than affection. They'd married more to assuage a mutual loneliness than because they felt a deep love.

What she felt for Devlin was nothing like her feelings for Bill. Her feelings for Devlin were so complex. She felt protected by him, but she also felt very protective of him. In his arms she felt safe, she also felt vividly alive.

Knowing how she felt didn't tell her how Devlin felt. that was the question that nagged at her now that she'd realized her own feelings.

He cared for her—that much she was aware of. But whether that caring went deeper than the concern he'd feel for anyone who was down on their luck, she couldn't be sure.

One thing she knew was that he had an enormous amount to give, if only he was willing to do so. It didn't take a psychic to tell her that he was wary of involvement. That he'd gotten as involved with her as he had was a hopeful sign.

Be patient, Reed had said. Patience was one thing she had plenty of. She was willing to give Devlin all the time in the world to realize that they could build something together, something as strong and lasting as the house on which he was lavishing such care.

She'd wait as long as it took for him to realize the future would be much brighter if they faced it together.

But the future was rushing in much faster than Annalise realized.

"You look pale." Devlin's dark brows drew together as he frowned across the table at her.

"Thanks." When his expression didn't lighten, she let her smile fade. "I'm just a little tired."

"You were tired yesterday and the day before."

"Excuse me for being human," she snapped. Immediately she bit her lower lip, regretting the outburst. "I'm sorry."

"That's okay." His eyes were concerned. "You just seem a little out of sorts, that's all."

Annalise poked her fork listlessly into the chef's salad in front of her. While she'd been making it, she'd felt positively ravenous and had nibbled at the ham and cheese. Now that it was in front of her, it had lost its appeal. Maybe she'd nibbled more than she'd realized.

"I'm just tired," she repeated, summoning up a smile. Actually it was all she could do to keep her eyes open lately.

"You slept this afternoon," he pointed out, still frowning.

Annalise kept her lashes lowered, forcing back the sudden tears that stung her eyes. He wasn't being critical. He was concerned. It was wonderful that he cared enough to be concerned. So why did she feel like bursting into tears?

"Maybe I need to take more vitamins," she suggested, keeping her tone light.

"Maybe you need to see a doctor."

"I'm not sick." Her fork clattered on the table as she pushed her barely touched salad away. "It's probably just the heat."

"It hasn't been that hot."

"Well, maybe I think it's hot," she snapped, shoving back from the table.

Devlin watched her storm from the room. After a moment, he got up and began clearing the table. He hadn't talked to Ben Masters since telling him that Annalise was going to be staying with him for a day or two. He stacked the salad plates in the dishwasher and shut the door, his expression thoughtful.

He wasn't much inclined toward interfering in someone else's life. But he'd been noticing Annalise's unusual lethargy for a week now, since not long after Reed left. She slept later in the morning, went to bed earlier in the evenings and had taken more than one nap in the middle of the day.

It wouldn't hurt to call Ben and ask him to suggest a doctor—a woman. Not because he had felt any reluctance to have Annalise see a male doctor—no, that wasn't it at all. He just thought Annalise might be more comfortable with a woman.

Annalise was lying on the bed when he entered the bedroom. Beauty was seated beside her, getting her ears scratched. Two of the kittens were playing a game of tag on the bedspread.

"How are you feeling?" he asked quietly.

"Stupid." She stopped petting the cat and sat up, giving Devlin an apologetic smile. "I must be more tired than I thought to snap at you like that. I'm sorry."

"Don't worry about it." He came over to sit on the edge of the bed, drawing one knee up so that he faced her. "Before you get too much in sympathy with me, I should warn you that I called Ben Masters and got a recommendation for a doctor."

"Ben Masters. He's the doctor who was here the night you rescued me from the river, isn't he?"

"Yes." He'd been prepared for her to be furious. Instead, she looked thoughtful. "He suggested that you see a Dr. Linden. He says she's very good. I think I've heard Kelly mention her. Maybe you could call and ask her."

"That's okay. I'll trust your friend." She sighed. "I suppose it won't hurt to see a doctor. I'm sure there's nothing wrong that some vitamins won't cure."

"Sure." Devlin reached out to brush her hair back from her face, feeling a vague ache somewhere in the region of his heart. She looked so pale.

Maybe he was overreacting. No doubt she was right—she was probably just a little anemic. Woman got anemic all the time, right? But he couldn't deny that he'd feel better when the doctor confirmed it.

Devlin went with Annalise to Dr. Linden's office, though she insisted that she was perfectly capable of driving into Remembrance by herself. He had other things to do in town, he said vaguely. There was no reason to take two cars.

Secretly she rather liked having him with her. It made it seem as if they were a couple, as if there were more definite ties between them than he'd willingly admit existed. Besides, though she hadn't admitted as much, the blanket of exhaustion that seemed to be weighing her down lately had begun to worry her a little.

Dr. Linden was a pleasant woman in her forties. She had medium brown hair, lightly sprinkled with gray and rather ordinary features. But her brown eyes were kind and reassuring.

Annalise endured the examination and answered all the questions she were asked. By the time the nurse told her she could get dressed, she was starting to feel foolish for having come in. Really, a spell of tiredness didn't seem like a symptom worthy of taking up a doctor's time.

It was wonderful that Devlin had been concerned about her, but she shouldn't have let his concern push her into making an appointment that her better judgment told her was unnecessary. She got dressed, feeling as if she should apologize to the doctor.

But Dr. Linden didn't seem to feel any apology was necessary. The nurse showed Annalise into a pleasantly decorated office and told her to have a seat. She had only a moment to wait before the doctor came in and sat behind the desk. She spoke before Annalise could launch into the apologetic speech she'd been rehearsing.

"I think the source of your tiredness is obvious, Annalise."

"You do?" The question reflected her surprise. "What's wrong?"

"Nothing is wrong precisely." Dr. Linden folded her hands on top of Annalise's file and fixed the younger woman with a kind smile. "You're pregnant."

The words hit with sledgehammer force. Annalise stared at the doctor, her mind completely blank for the space of several heartbeats.

"I can't be."

"About eight weeks along, I'd say." Dr. Linden glanced at her notes again, giving her patient a chance to absorb the news.

"You're mistaken." There was absolute conviction behind the statement.

"You seem very sure of that."

"I can't have children."

Dr. Linden's brows rose in surprise. "It says here that you had a successful pregnancy." She glanced at the chart for confirmation.

"Yes, but the doctors told me it was virtually a miracle that I got pregnant that one time." She explained, calmly and thoroughly, just why it was that she couldn't be pregnant.

For one moment, when the doctor had said she was pregnant, she'd felt a fierce blaze of joy, but she'd controlled it immediately, knowing that there'd been a mistake.

Dr. Linden listened to her explanation politely, asking one or two questions to clarify the situation.

"So you understand why there's been a mistake," Annalise finished, trying to pretend that her chest wasn't so tight with pain that she could hardly breathe.

"I understand why you find it difficult to believe, Annalise, but I'd like to point out that medicine is not as exact a science as we'd all like it to be. Certainly, the conditions you're describing would make conception extremely difficult—almost impossible. But it's that 'almost' that's the key word here. You did conceive once."

"But they said it was a miracle," Annalise whispered, terrified to let herself start believing that what the doctor had told her could be true—that she could be carrying Devlin's baby.

"It's possible to have two miracles in one lifetime," Dr. Linden said gently. "You seem to have been twice blessed."

Looking at her, Annalise felt the reality of it start to sink in. A baby. She was going to have another baby. Devlin's baby. Tears filled her eyes. She pressed her hand over her flat stomach, letting the miracle slowly become real.

* * *

When she rejoined Devlin in the waiting room, she had to swallow the urge to shout out the news. She'd stuffed all the brochures and pamphlets she'd been given into her purse and decided that tomorrow would be soon enough to fill the prescription for prenatal vitamins. At the moment, vitamins weren't as important as going home and breaking the news to Devlin that he was going to be a father.

She told him that the doctor had given her a clean bill of health—which wasn't a lie. A pregnancy wasn't the same thing as an illness. Devlin's relief was obvious and Annalise hugged that to her on the drive home.

Surely he couldn't be so concerned about her and not have deep feelings for her. Deep enough to want to have a child with her?

He'd once said that he would never be a father. She hadn't pursued the subject. It hadn't seemed relevant. How could she have known that it was going to become suddenly, wonderfully, very relevant?

Annalise was so absorbed in both savoring the miracle of carrying a child and worrying about Devlin's reaction to the news that she didn't notice the increasingly worried looks he threw her as they neared home.

He waited until they'd entered the house before speaking.

"What did Dr. Linden really say?" he asked abruptly. He tossed his keys onto the breakfast bar and turned to look at her, his shoulders taut.

"I told you what she said." Annalise set her purse down, keeping her face averted from his. She needed time to decide how to tell him.

"But that's not all she said, is it?"

She glanced at him, reading the concern in his eyes. Looking away, she nibbled on her lower lip. Obviously he'd picked up on her distraction. He thought she was concealing something from him and he was right. But it wasn't what he thought. Maybe this was the best time to tell him after all.

"Do you remember that I told you I couldn't have children, that getting pregnant with Mary was practically a miracle?"

"Yes. What's wrong? Do you need surgery?"

"No. Actually, nothing's wrong exactly." She swallowed hard and linked her hands together to control the trembling of her fingers. She met his eyes, her own shining with joy. "I'm pregnant."

"What?" Devlin stared at her, his expression as blank as she'd felt when Dr. Linden first told her the news.

"I'm pregnant," she said again, her voice trembling with happiness. "We're going to have a baby, Devlin."

This time, the words penetrated. Annalise saw their impact in his eyes. She held her breath. She was prepared for him to be angry. They'd never even discussed the possibility of having a future together, and suddenly they were going to be parents. Even in the midst of her own delight, she wasn't foolish enough to assume that Devlin was going to instantaneously find the same joy in his impending fatherhood.

Emotion flashed across his face, but it was gone too quickly for her to read, leaving his eyes slate gray and completely empty of expression.

"Is your health all right?" he asked in a neutral tone.

"Yes. The doctor says I'm fine." Her eyes searched his face, trying to read something behind the blank facade he'd put up. "Devlin..."

"I'm glad you're well," he interrupted without apology. He glanced at his watch. "I forgot to pick up some things in town. I'd better get going or it'll be too late. Is there anything you need me to pick up?"

"I... I have a prescription for vitamins," she said slowly, feeling as if she'd missed a part of the conversation somewhere.

"I'll fill it at Johnson's."

Since he seemed to be expecting it, she got her purse and found the prescription. He took it from her and put it into his shirt pocket without looking at it. "Is there anything else you need?" He might have been a room service waiter asking if she had everything she needed before he left the room.

She shook her head. Devlin nodded politely and picked up his keys. A moment later, the door shut behind him, leaving her alone.

That appeared to be the end of matter, as far as Devlin was concerned. For three days, Annalise waited for him to mention the baby, waited for him to show some emotion about it. Anger, dislike, even hatred. Anything would have been better than the complete indifference he seemed to feel.

She couldn't complain about his treatment of her. He was perfectly polite. He inquired after her health each day. He thanked her for the meals she prepared, meals neither of them ate more than a few mouthfuls of.

He also came to bed every night after she was asleep and was up before she woke. His eyes never did more than skim across her face, as if he couldn't bear to look at her.

She told herself he needed time to adjust to the idea. It had been as big a shock to him as it had to her. Where she could greet the news of her pregnancy with unadulterated joy, it was understandable that his feelings were not so simple.

Time, that was what he needed. Once he'd gotten over the shock, they'd be able to talk about the baby. They'd be able to decide what lay in the future. Annalise never had a moment's concern that he'd refuse to help her in caring for the child. She knew Devlin well enough to know that he'd take his responsibility seriously.

But she wanted their child to be more than a responsibility. She wanted Devlin to want this baby as much as she did. If she just gave him a little time to come to terms with the news, everything would be all right.

After three days, when nothing had changed, she decided that perhaps time alone wasn't going to do it. If there'd been only herself to consider, she might have packed a bag and left, no matter how much it tore her heart to shreds to leave him. But it wasn't just her anymore.

She had a child to consider now, and she had to try to make the child's father understand just what an incredible miracle they'd been given.

"We need to talk." She hadn't planned on it coming out so abruptly. She'd planned on approaching the subject more obliquely, but it was hard to be oblique with a man who was doing a damned good job of avoiding her.

"I have things to do." He had his hand on the doorknob and he didn't turn to look at her.

"We need to talk about the baby," she said determinedly.

Devlin's shoulders stiffened as if the word *baby* was a lash laid across them.

"I don't think so," he said tightly, still without turning.

"You can't just pretend it doesn't exist," Annalise threw at him.

His hand dropped from the doorknob and he turned slowly, looking at her without expression. "I'm not pretending it doesn't exist."

"Aren't you? You haven't mentioned it."

"Perhaps that's because I have nothing to say."

"You're going to be a father," she said, her tone pleading.

"No!" The facade of indifference vanished in an instant, revealing a blazing anger that made his eyes almost silver. "That's something I will never be!"

Annalise gripped her hands together. She lifted her chin. "You can't possibly think this isn't your baby."

"No. I know you conceived it with me." He made it sound like a cold, clinical act, and Annalise felt hurt rise inside her.

"Then how can you say you're not the father?"

"I'm the father, but it won't be anything more than an empty title." He stepped away from the door, facing her, his eyes full of anger. "You don't have to worry that I won't support you. I'll make sure you and your child have everything you need. But that's as far as it's going to go."

Her child. The words made it clear that he was distancing himself as much as possible. She fought the urge to turn away from his anger, to give in to the tears that burned at the back of her eyes. Anger wasn't going to do them any good. God knows, he had enough for the two of them.

"Can't we talk about this?" She struggled for a reasonable tone.

"Talk? What shall we talk about?" he asked nastily. "Shall we talk about how you lied to me? How you told me you couldn't get pregnant?"

"I didn't lie!" She was shocked by the accusation. In all her thinking, it had never occurred to her that he might believe she'd lied about her inability to conceive.

"Pardon me if I find that a little hard to believe," he sneered.

"It's the truth! Why would I lie about that?"

"Because you wanted me to get you knocked up," he said crudely. "Because you wanted a baby to replace the one you lost."

Annalise wasn't even aware that she'd moved until she saw her hand arcing through the air. Her palm hit his cheek with enough force to jerk his head to the side. The sound of the slap echoed in the big house.

Her hand fell to her side. He looked at her, the imprint of her hand scarlet on his cheek.

"You got what you wanted," he said. "You've got your baby. I'll make sure you're taken care of, but I don't see any reason to smile about it."

She stared at him, seeing the deep anger he felt. At another time, she might have seen the fear that underlay the anger, but her own emotions were too tumultuous for her to see anything but the obvious, which was that he was looking at her as if he hated her.

Shaken and trembling, Annalise was incapable of putting together the words to defend herself. That he could believe she'd use him as he'd just said, cut to the bone.

When he turned and walked out, she didn't try to stop him. She stood frozen in place, listening to the roar of the truck's engine disappearing down the driveway. He was going too fast, she thought vaguely. He'd spin out in the gravel at the bottom of the driveway. But he'd get it under control again. Devlin always got things under control again.

Moving dazedly, she turned and went into the bedroom. Methodically she began removing her clothes from the closet. Beauty, sensing that all was not as it should be, leaped up onto the bed and sat down on top of the small stack of garments. Looking up at Annalise, she meowed inquiringly.

Annalise felt the ice that had encased her crack. Sinking onto the bed, she scooped the cat up in her arms. Rocking back and forth, she let the tears start. In the past few minutes, not only her world but her heart had shattered into a thousand pieces.

And she didn't know if she'd be able to put either back together.

Chapter 13

Devlin took the turn at the end of the driveway too quickly. The rear wheels slid on the loose gravel. His hands tightened on the wheel, and he wrenched the truck into line with brute force.

The road was, as usual, empty. It was just as well, because Devlin sent the truck down it as if all the demons in hell were speeding after him. The trouble was, he was carrying the demons with him. No matter how fast he went, he couldn't escape them. Instead of the country road in front of him, he saw Annalise's white face, the hurt in her eyes. The image made it hurt to draw a breath.

Cursing, he slowed the truck, pulling it off to the side of the road. His hands knotted on the steering wheel, he stared through the windshield.

He'd been a fool. Annalise was no more capable of using him to get her pregnant than she was of swimming the English Channel. He couldn't remember ever hearing her tell a lie. He'd wanted—needed—to believe that she'd lied to him, that she'd used him.

From the moment she'd told him that she was pregnant, he'd felt torn apart by conflicting emotions. There'd been a part of him that had felt utter joy. A child was something he'd never thought to have, and he'd told himself he felt no regrets at that decision. But when he pictured Annalise carrying his baby, holding his son or daughter in her arms, he'd realized how wrong he'd been to think it was something he didn't want.

But the joy was quickly swallowed up by fear. He didn't have to close his eyes to see his father standing over him, his thin face twisted with hatred, his belt raised. He'd sworn never to have a child, never to risk finding that insanity in himself.

And suddenly, there was Annalise, telling him she was carrying his child, making him confront his own worst nightmares. His reaction had been rage. He'd told himself that it was rage because she'd lied, because she'd used him. In reality, the anger was easier to deal with than the fear that boiled like acid inside him.

But that didn't give him the right to hurt her. What if she left?

He stared down the empty country road, seeing his life stretch ahead of him, equally empty, equally lonely. Since Annalise had come into his life, he'd known a contentment, a happiness, he'd never thought himself capable of feeling.

She'd had a childhood scarcely less painful than his own. Her marriage had broken up just when she'd needed support the most, and she'd had to stand by and watch a beloved child die. And she hadn't let any of it destroy her. Perhaps it had come close, he thought, remembering the lifeless woman he'd pulled from the river.

But all she'd needed was a little time, a little bit of security, and she'd pulled her life back together. She'd not only learned to laugh again, she'd taught him how to laugh. She'd opened her heart to Beauty and Lobo—and one Devlin Russell—unwanted strays, all of them.

She'd given them all a home. Not just a house but a home. He'd thought he was building a home this past year, but now he could see what he'd really been doing was building himself a wall to keep the world at bay. Another prison, only this one was to protect him from life—from living.

If she left, it would be like hearing those big iron doors slide shut behind him. Only this time, there would be no reprieve, no one to say he wasn't guilty after all. He'd have no one to blame but himself.

His fingers were not quite steady as he turned the key in the ignition. He had to talk to her, apologize. God, how could he offer an apology for the things he'd said to her? He'd been unforgivably cruel. But whether she forgave him or not, she had a right to hear the apology.

He drove back at the same breakneck pace at which he'd left. He had no idea how long he'd been sitting there staring at the empty fields, realizing what a fool he'd been. She could have had time to pack and leave by now.

If she was gone, he'd just have to find her, he told himself. He'd track her down no matter where she'd gone and tell her he was sorry. She'd no doubt kick him out of her life, but he couldn't let her think that he really believed the things he'd accused her of.

Her car was still beside the house, and Devlin felt the band around his chest ease slightly. She wasn't gone yet. He could talk to her, tell her how sorry he was, tell her he hadn't meant any of it.

He strode into the house, trying to think of what he was going to say to her. How did you begin to apologize for the kind of things he'd said? But he had to find the words. He owed her that much.

Annalise was in the bedroom. He felt an almost paralyzing stab of pain when he saw what she was doing. Her clothes were on the bed. She was folding them neatly and setting them in a cardboard box. The same damned box they'd been in when he towed her car home, he realized.

She glanced up, her eyes not quite touching on his still figure, settling somewhere just to the left of him instead.

"I'm almost done. I thought you'd be gone longer." There was no anger in her tone. No hurt. There was nothing there at all. She could have been talking to a stranger.

"Annalise, I'm sorry." He winced at the inadequacy of the words, but they were all he had to offer.

"That's quite all right," she said politely. She folded a pair of jeans and set them in the box. "Actually, it's probably just as well you did come back. I was hoping it would be all right if I left Beauty and the kittens here, just until I find an apartment. I know you didn't particularly want a cat and I'll take her off your hands as soon as possible."

"Fine." He watched as she took a blouse off a hanger and began folding it. He felt as if he were breaking into a hundred tiny pieces inside.

"Lobo, too, if you'd like," she went on, setting the blouse on top of the jeans. "Although, he really considers himself more yours than mine. If you want, I'll take him, too. I don't want you to feel as if you're stuck with him."

Where did she think she was going to find an apartment that would let her have, not only a cat and four kittens, but a dog the size of a Shetland pony?

"He can stay. You can all stay."

"No!" For an instant, her careful calm wavered and her fingers knotted over the T-shirt she'd just picked up. "Thank you," she said politely, forcing her fingers to relax.

"I was wrong."

"Yes, you were." But there was no anger in her words.

"I know you didn't lie to me about thinking you couldn't have children. I think I knew all along."

"I'm glad." She folded the last garment and set it in the box. "Excuse me. I want to make sure I didn't leave anything in the bathroom."

Devlin watched her leave the bedroom, feeling a blackness rising up inside, threatening to swallow him whole. He couldn't let her leave like this. There were things that needed to be said.

She came back into the room with a bottle of shampoo in her hand and tucked it down along the side of the box. Her eyes skimmed over the room, as if checking to see if she'd missed anything. The fingers that rested on the sides of the box trembled slightly.

It was that trembling that gave him hope. He hadn't managed to kill her feelings for him completely if the thought of leaving could make her tremble.

"Don't go."

The simple plea sounded loud in the quiet room. Annalise closed her eyes as if the words had a physical impact.

"Don't," she said softly. "I understand how you feel."

"Do you?"

"Yes. You made it clear you didn't want a child. You didn't truly want to get involved with me, did you?" For the first time, she squarely looked at him, her mouth quirked in a half smile. "I guess I shouldn't have thought that because you made an exception on one, you'd be able to make an exception on the other. A baby is a much bigger commitment than a lover, isn't it?"

"I didn't want to get involved," he admitted slowly. He tried to pick his words carefully. This might be the only chance he had to make her understand, to beg her forgiveness. "I've always known that I'd never have a serious relationship with a woman. I never thought I was capable of the kind of feelings that required."

"Oh, Devlin." Annalise looked at him, the compassion in her eyes sending a stab of pain through him. "You're capable of a great deal more than you give yourself credit for. I've never met anyone with so much to give. Look at the way you took me in. And Beauty and Lobo. Strays, all of us," she said, unknowingly echoing his earlier thoughts. "You shouldn't sell yourself short."

He felt hope surge up. Surely she couldn't look at him like that, say that he had so much to give and not still feel something for him.

"Annalise, I—"

"I should get going." She looked away from him, her tone suddenly brisk. "I need to find a motel tonight."

"Please. Don't go."

Her finger knotted over the sides of the box. She felt a wave of pain wash over her. He sounded as if he meant it. There was need in his voice, in his eyes. She wanted desperately to respond to that need, but she couldn't.

Her chest still ached with the pain of his earlier words. He felt badly about having hurt her and he wanted a chance to make it right. But the only thing that could make it right was if he loved her. And he didn't. He couldn't have loved her and said those things to her.

"I have to go," she said tightly. "I accept your apology, but I have to go."

"I was afraid," he told her, taking a step away from the doorway.

"Afraid? Of what?" Despite herself, her eyes went to his face. She didn't want to listen to him, didn't want to care about what he had to say.

"Of being hurt."

"So you thought you'd strike first?"

"Of hurting you," he continued, ignoring her sharp question. "Of hurting the . . . the child."

"You did hurt me," she told him, anger and pain tangled together in her stomach.

"I don't mean that kind of hurt." He waved one hand in an impatient gesture.

"What other kind of hurt is . . ." Her voice trailed off. She stared at him, suddenly realizing what he meant. He was talking about physical hurt. Maybe she should have thought of it before, considering what he'd told her of his childhood.

"You think you might hit me or our child?" she asked, incredulity colouring her tone.

"The capability is there."

"Nonsense." There was no hesitation in her brisk denial. "You're no more capable of hurting someone smaller than you than you are of . . . of leaping tall buildings in a single bound."

Devlin blinked at her, disconcerted by her instantaneous dismissal of a fear that had haunted him all his life.

"My father..."

"Your father was obviously a very sick man, but I don't think it was a genetic illness."

"I could..."

"No, you couldn't." She sounded so completely sure. Devlin stared at her, feeling her confidence nudge at the base of the fear lodged inside him. "I know all the statistics about abused children becoming abusive parents, but it doesn't happen every time, Devlin. You couldn't ever become a child abuser."

He shoved his hands into his pockets and half turned away, ashamed of the tears that burned in his eyes. Once again, her belief in him made him feel strong and, at the same time, achingly weak.

Annalise watched him, feeling some of her pain ease in the face of his. He truly believed he could have it in him to hurt his child the way his father had hurt him. No wonder he'd been so adamant about never being a father.

He'd hurt her deeply with his accusations. That pain couldn't be completely wiped away because she now understood his motives. But her love for him couldn't be so easily destroyed, either. Through her own hurt, she felt his pain.

"Devlin, you'd be a wonderful father," she said softly. "I've always known that."

"Have you?" He turned to look at her. His eyes dropped to her stomach for a moment before lifting to her face. "Am I going to get a chance to find out?"

It was her turn to look away. She loved him. With all her heart, she wanted him to be a part of their child's life. A part of her life. But they couldn't go on as they had been, playing at house without some sort of commitment. She wanted to bring her child into a stable home, full of warmth. Full of love.

The old saying about half a loaf being better than none might apply to bread, but it didn't apply to love. Not for her. She'd thought she could go on indefinitely, waiting for him to see what they could have together. Maybe she could have if she hadn't gotten pregnant. But the baby changed everything.

"I want it all," she said softly. "I want a commitment. I want to know that you'll still be here no matter how rough it gets. I want to know that...that you love me as much as I love you."

She lifted her chin, her eyes meeting his with fierce pride.

Devlin felt his heart stop. She loved him. She loved him. Suddenly his heart was beating much too fast, making him feel almost light-headed. He'd never realized how desperately he wanted to hear those three little words from her. He'd never let himself realize how much he needed her to say them.

"Annalise." He took a step toward her and stopped. He took his hands out of his pockets and reached for hers. She let him take her hands, but there was no give in her. He'd always known there was strength in her. It was part of what he'd admired from the start. It had never been more evident than it was at this minute.

"Annalise, I never planned on getting involved with a woman. I never thought I could...love anyone."

"Of course you can." Her fingers squeezed his. "If you'll just let yourself."

He stared down at their linked hands, searching for the words to make her understand. "I care for you," he said slowly. "Wait." His fingers tightened over hers, preventing her from pulling away. "I know that doesn't sound like much, but it's more than I ever thought I'd feel for someone."

"I know," she said softly, without anger. "But I need more than that."

"I want to wake up beside you every morning," he told her. He lifted his eyes to her face. "I want to know that you're there when I wake up in the middle of the night. I want to watch your stomach grow with our child. I want to be there when that child is born. I want to know that you'll always be there, no matter what."

He drew her closer, desperate to make her understand how much he needed her in his life. "You have to stay, Annalise. Without you, I . . . don't know what I'd do."

She looked at him, feeling the last traces of ice melt from around her heart. The words he couldn't seem to get out were written in his eyes. He loved her. It was there in the way he held her hands, in the near desperation in his eyes.

She freed one hand, reaching up to lay it against his jaw. "You're talking about love, Devlin. You're talking about needing someone else to make your life complete. About wanting to share the bad, as well as the good. What do you think love is?"

"I don't know," he said simply. She knew it was no less than the truth. How could he know? There'd been so little of it in his life.

"Oh, Devlin." She leaned into him, resting her cheek against his chest, feeling the strong beat of his heart. His arms closed convulsively around her, and he bent to put his face against her hair.

"Teach me, Annalise," he whispered. "I don't want to lose you."

"You're not going to." She tilted her head to look up into his face. "You're stuck with me."

"We'll get married."

"I'd like that," she said, seeing some of the anxiety fade from his eyes.

He didn't need her to teach him how to love. All she needed to teach him was that he didn't have to be afraid to love. As long as she could see the love in his eyes, she could wait for the words. They weren't as important as feeling his arms around her, holding her as if he'd never let her go.

* * * * *

NORA ROBERTS

THE LANGUAGE of LOVE

Silhouette Special Edition

is pleased to present

A GOOD MAN WALKS IN
by Ginna Gray

The story of one strong woman's comeback
and the man who was there for her, Travis McCall,
the renegade cousin to those Blaine siblings,
from Ginna Gray's bestselling trio

FOOLS RUSH IN (#416)
WHERE ANGELS FEAR (#468)
ONCE IN A LIFETIME (#661)

Rebecca Quinn sought shelter at the hideaway on Rincon
Island. Finding Travis McCall—the object of all her childhood
crushes—holed up in the same house threatened to ruin the
respite she so desperately needed. Until their first kiss . . .
Then Travis set out to prove to his lovely Rebecca that man
can be good and love, sublime.

You'll want to be there when Rebecca's disillusionment turns
to joy.

A GOOD MAN WALKS IN #722

Available at your favorite retail outlet this February.

Silhouette Romance®

LONG, TALL TEXANS

DONAVAN
Diana Palmer

Diana Palmer's bestselling LONG, TALL TEXANS series continues with DONAVAN....

From the moment elegant Fay York walked into the bar on the wrong side of town, rugged Texan Donavan Langley knew she was trouble. But the lovely young innocent awoke a tenderness in him that he'd never known...and a desire to make her a proposal she couldn't refuse....

Don't miss DONAVAN by Diana Palmer, the ninth book in her LONG, TALL TEXANS series. Coming in January...only from Silhouette Romance.

LTT192

Take 4 bestselling love stories FREE

Plus get a FREE surprise gift!

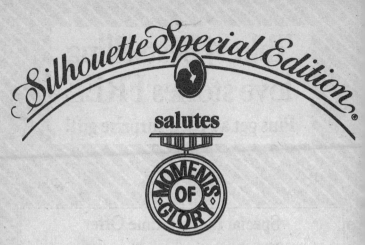

Silhouette Special Edition®

salutes

MOMENTS OF GLORY

from Lindsay McKenna

In a country torn with conflict, in a time of bitter passions, these brave men and women wage a war against all odds . . . and a timeless battle for honor, for fleeting moments of glory, for the promise of enduring love.

February: RIDE THE TIGER (#721) Survivor Dany Villard is wise to the love-'em-and-leave-'em ways of war, but wounded hero Gib Ramsey swears she's captured his heart . . . forever.

March: ONE MAN'S WAR (#727) The war raging inside brash and bold Captain Pete Mallory threatens to destroy him, until Tess Ramsey's tender love guides him toward peace.

April: OFF LIMITS (#733) Soft-spoken Marine Jim McKenzie saved Alexandra Vance's life in Vietnam; now he needs her love to save his honor. . . .

SEMG-1